THIS BOOK BELONGS TO:

_____

_____

Also in this series:

SHOWTYM ADVENTURES

CASPER, THE SPIRITED ARABIAN

KELLY WILSON

SHOWTYM ADVENTURES

CASPER,
THE SPIRITED ARABIAN

PUFFIN

UK | USA | Canada | Ireland | Australia
India | New Zealand | South Africa | China

Puffin is an imprint of the Penguin Random House group of companies, whose addresses
can be found at global.penguinrandomhouse.com.

Penguin
Random House
New Zealand

First published by Penguin Random House New Zealand, 2018

10 9 8 7 6 5 4 3 2 1

Text © Kelly Wilson, 2018

Design by Cat Taylor © Penguin Random House New Zealand
Author photo by Amanda Wilson
Illustrations by Heather Wilson © Penguin Random House New Zealand
Cover illustrations by Jenny Cooper © Penguin Random House New Zealand

Printed and bound in Australia by Griffin Press, an Accredited ISO AS/NZS 14001
Environmental Management Systems Printer

A catalogue record for this book is available from the National Library of New Zealand.

ISBN 978-0-14-377224-8
eISBN 978-0-14-377225-5

penguin.co.nz

MIX
Paper | Supporting
responsible forestry
FSC® C018684

This book is dedicated to our horses and ponies, both past and present, especially the difficult ones. Every single horse that has crossed our paths has taught us something new, and we wouldn't be the same without them.

Thank you for constantly challenging us to learn more, to always question how we can improve our horses' quality of life, and for loving us even with our imperfections.

Some of our best friends over the years have been horses, and almost all of our favourite adventures have included our four-legged partners in crime.

Growing up, we Wilson sisters — Vicki, Amanda and me (I'm Kelly) — were three ordinary girls with a love of horses and dreams of Grand Prix show jumping, taming wild horses and becoming world champions.

In *Showtym Adventures*, we want to share stories based on our early years with ponies, to inspire you to have big dreams, too! I hope you enjoy reading about the special ponies that started us on our journey...

Love,
   Kelly

Contents

Chapter 1
Nightmare Pony

"WHAT DO YOU MEAN BY DANGEROUS?" Vicki asked, glancing over at her friend Stella in concern. The girls were discussing their favourite topic during school break: ponies. Stella had been looking for her dream pony for months now, and Vicki was always eager to hear how the search was going. But even Vicki, who had been obsessed with horses and riding for all of the eleven years of her life, found it hard to keep track of the ponies her friend had tried. "That's the grey Arabian, right?"

"Yeah," Stella sighed. "We couldn't even enter his

paddock." She flipped her long blonde hair over her shoulder and nibbled at a sandwich. "As soon as he saw us, he laid his ears back and charged. I was so glad we were on the other side of the fence."

"So not the pony of your dreams, then?" Vicki said with a laugh.

"Maybe one from my nightmares," Stella giggled, just as the bell rang. "The owner doesn't want much money for him, but even so, no one's interested. I can understand why!"

Grabbing her lunch-box and stuffing it back into her bag, Stella rose to her feet. "His name is Casper, but he's not a friendly ghost. He's the most unfriendly pony I've ever met."

"It certainly sounds like he's got himself a bad reputation," Vicki replied.

U U U

A few days later, Vicki went from job to job on their little farm, with her younger sisters, trying to keep busy. First they cleaned out the bird aviary and laid clean hay in the rabbit boxes, then they mucked out their ponies' paddocks and cleaned their gear.

Since the show season had finished a couple of weeks earlier, their ponies were having a month's holiday from being ridden. Vicki missed riding so much — she couldn't help but feel that there wasn't much fun to be had on the weekends now. Her thoughts drifted back to the last time she'd ridden at an event.

"What are you smiling about?"

Vicki, jolted from her thoughts, turned to see that her six-year-old sister Amanda had paused in the act of scrubbing her pony's bit, and was looking at her inquisitively.

"I'm just reliving my last hunter class event on Dandy at the Royal Easter Show. I still can't believe we won Champion!"

"It was the best show," nine-year-old Kelly reflected as she cleaned her pony's saddle. "I was so proud of how well Cameo went. She jumped like she'd been competing for years! No one even guessed she'd only been ridden for the first time at the start of the season."

"Charlie was great, too," Amanda grinned proudly, showing off her missing front tooth. "No riding on the lead rein for me!"

"All our ponies were amazing, which makes me miss competing even more." Vicki sighed, and hung up her well-oiled bridle. "We have four months until the show season starts again. We need to plan an adventure soon, otherwise the winter is going to seem endless."

"What do you have in mind?" Kelly asked, clearly just as keen for some fun.

"Something to do with horses obviously, but that's the problem — I can't think of anything. Well, anything that doesn't involve spending a heap of money that we don't have."

As Vicki helped her sisters finish the last of their chores, her mind whirled. She was feeling restless and bored. The problem with Dandy having a holiday, she realised, was that she didn't know what to do with herself if she couldn't ride.

"I'm missing you," Vicki whispered to the chestnut gelding, as she covered him for the night. "We need to come up with a new project to make the winter go quickly."

Vicki's mum noticed that she was unusually quiet at dinner.

"Vicki, what's on your mind?" she asked.

"I'm trying to plan an adventure," Vicki said, as she moved the food around on her plate. "With the ponies on holiday, the weekends have all been the same lately. Kelly, Amanda and I were trying to think of something fun we can do."

"Well, we can't go too far afield, but what about a day trip?" Dad suggested.

"Where would we go?" Amanda asked.

"Anywhere you like. We could visit the waterfalls, or go hiking in the bush, or even go caving?"

"I was hoping it could be something to do with horses," Vicki admitted with a sigh.

"If you can think of somewhere that's under an hour's drive and involves horses, then we're all ears," her dad said.

All of a sudden, a thought began to form in Vicki's mind. She smiled and sat up straighter in her chair.

"Each weekend, Stella's been trying different ponies to buy, and it sounds really fun. How about we look at horses for sale in the local paper, and we go and try the first one listed? We don't have to buy it, but it'll be fun looking. And we might even get to ride!"

"I know that people often visit houses for sale, but I've never thought of doing it with horses for sale!" Mum laughed. "That actually sounds like fun." She reached for the newspaper. Flicking through the pages, she found the Horses for Sale section and read out the first listing. "*14.2hh 6-year-old grey Arabian gelding. Needs experienced home. $250.*"

Vicki's breath caught. Surely this must be the same pony Stella had looked at?

"Shall I give them a call?" Dad asked.

With a nod from all three girls, he reached for the phone and dialled the number.

"Hi, I'm ringing up about the pony you have for sale."

Vicki listened as her dad asked a few questions, and noticed the growing frown on his face. Now she was sure it must be the same pony.

"Would it suit you if we came out to look at him tomorrow?" Dad asked at last. Jotting down an address, he disconnected the call and looked at his daughters. "She's expecting us at 2 p.m."

"Really?" Vicki said in delight. "Was the pony called Casper, by any chance? It might be one Stella tried."

"I'm not sure, I never asked the pony's name." Looking at his wife, Dad shook his head. "You sure picked a winner. It sounds like a real terror."

"Just as well we're not looking to buy," Mum replied with a shrug. "Between us, four ponies are more than enough!"

Chapter 2
First Impressions

"I'D LIKE TO INTRODUCE YOU to Casper," the lady said, pointing to the far corner of the muddy paddock.

Vicki's eyes settled on a noticeably dirty and skinny grey pony. The gelding cocked an ear when he saw them, then snorted and took off at a gallop around the field. With his mane and tail flying in the wind he looked majestic, and Vicki couldn't help but see past his poor condition to admire the Arabian's dished head and refined features.

"He's beautiful," she said softly, as the pony

dropped back to an expressive trot and danced his way towards them.

"If only he had the personality to match," the lady sighed. "I bought him almost a year ago, but he's been much more difficult than I anticipated. I don't feel safe handling him anymore, let alone riding him."

"What does he do?" Mum asked, as she eyed the approaching gelding.

"Wait and see."

Sure enough, Casper's disposition rapidly changed as he drew closer to them. His ears, which had been pricked forward, now pinned back against his skull, and his muzzle pinched as he swiped his teeth towards them in warning.

"He's a real charmer," Mum said dryly. "How does he behave with other ponies?"

"He's the only horse I have on the property, but he was paddocked with others before I got him and seemed fine," the lady was quick to reassure. "He's a little better once the halter's on. Let me catch him for you."

Vicki watched as the pony's owner slung a halter over her shoulder and entered the paddock. As she

quietly approached, murmuring softly, Casper half-reared and bared his teeth again.

"Cut it out," she growled softly, as she reached out a hand to stroke him.

Tensely, the Arabian stood as the halter was secured on his head, then begrudgingly followed as he was led from his paddock.

"He threatens, but he hasn't actually bitten me yet," the lady said.

"In the wrong hands I'm sure he could turn really aggressive, though," Dad said quietly to Mum.

"He seems really angry," Amanda whispered as she watched Casper drag on the lead rope, his ears flattened.

"I wonder what's happened to make him so unhappy," Vicki mused as they followed the gelding back to his yard. The gorgeous grey had lost most of his fire; now that he was caught, he walked slowly, dragging on the lead rope. "What was he like before he came to you?"

"I bought Casper from the Arabian stud that bred him. They'd broken him in as a four-year-old and he'd been ridden for about a year. He was a little difficult when I tried him, but I just thought he was young and inexperienced. I hoped he'd improve with time, but sadly it hasn't worked out that way," the lady replied as she tied Casper up.

Vicki stepped a little closer to the pony. "Life hasn't been easy on you, has it?" she whispered to him.

Snorting, the gelding tossed his head away and eyed Vicki warily.

"Do you mind if I groom him for a while?" Vicki asked the lady, spying a brush.

"If it's all right with your parents, then I'm fine with it."

"Do you want me to hold him?" Dad offered.

"Oh no, Casper's much better one on one," the lady rushed to reply, holding up a hand. "He'll be easier if it's just the two of them."

For the next ten minutes, Vicki quietly brushed

the mud from Casper's hairy coat while her parents talked to the owner. Occasionally he would flick an ear forward, or lean into the brush, and although his disgruntled expression didn't change, Vicki was convinced the pony was enjoying the grooming session.

"I don't think you're as naughty as you pretend to be," she said, stepping closer to Casper. "It's all an act, isn't it?"

Reaching out to stroke him between the eyes, Vicki kept a close eye on Casper's expression. She didn't want to do anything to make the pony bite her. As her hand settled on his head she swept his forelock out of the way, then traced the double swirls on his forehead.

Blinking sleepily, Casper sighed.

"I don't think he wants to be bad," Vicki said, turning to her parents. "He seems sweet."

"Not the word most people would use to describe him," the lady laughed, a little despairingly. "Would you like to see him saddled, or try riding him?"

"He's probably not what we're looking for," Mum replied quickly, seeing a good chance to escape. "But thank you for your time."

Visibly disappointed, the lady nodded. "I've had more than twenty people look at him, and everyone's said exactly the same thing. I'm not sure what I'm going to do with him. I can't keep him forever."

"Come on, Mum," Vicki begged. "Let's at least give him a proper chance. Please, Dad?"

Dad hesitated. "I guess we could see him saddled," he said with an apologetic glance at Mum, "but then we really should get going."

As soon as the lady approached with the saddle, Casper was wide awake again. Tugging on the lead, he backed up, spinning away to avoid the saddle being placed on his back. When it was time to do the girth up he was even more agitated.

"Is he always that bad?" Vicki asked as she watched the miserable pony.

"Worse, sometimes," his owner replied, her face creased in concern. "And he's just as bad to bridle. Sometimes I wonder if he's even safe to re-home."

"Oh, no, surely you'll find someone to love him?" Vicki gasped.

"That's what I'm hoping for," the lady said. "But if I can't find someone willing to give him a chance soon, I'm going to be out of options."

Chapter 3
No More Ponies

THE CAR RIDE HOME was much quieter than their drive to view the pony, and it was Amanda who eventually broke the oppressive silence.

"That was the saddest pony I've ever seen."

"Me too," Kelly whispered. "I hope someone saves him."

Looking out the window with a heavy heart, Vicki thought back over her encounter with the stroppy Arabian. She knew what she had to do.

"Mum, Dad, please can we buy him?"

Her mother whipped her head around and

gasped, "Vicki, you can't be serious. We had an agreement that we were just going to *look* at ponies, not buy one."

"Mum, I know we did, but he might be put down if nobody takes him. And there's good in him, I know it. He just needs someone to believe in him."

"What would you even *do* with him? There's no guarantee he's going to improve, and even if he does, it's unlikely he'll be any good for competing, or be safe to sell on."

"Your mum's right," Dad said. "Besides all those things, we can't afford to look after another pony."

Frustrated but undeterred, Vicki fell silent, thinking hard.

"What would it take," she began again, "for me to convince you that Casper is worth saving?"

"Vicki, we don't need another pony," Mum sighed.

"What about as a good deed?" Vicki said. "What if, by our giving him a chance, he's able to enjoy life again? That would be reward enough."

"But it's not going to pay the bills," Dad said, as he steered the car into their driveway. "Owning an extra pony costs money, and you know there's not a lot to spare at the moment."

U U U

That night as Vicki lay in bed, her mind flashed back to Casper. She didn't know what he'd been through in his short life, but she was sure she could win his trust and offer him a better future. The only ones standing in the way were her parents.

"I'm willing to take a chance on him," Vicki begged her mum, as they drove to school the next day. "But I need you to take a chance on me."

"It's not that I doubt your good intentions," Mum said, stopping the car outside the school entrance. "But we can't save every sad pony we come across."

"But he's only *one* pony," Amanda pointed out, as she slung her school bag over her shoulder and climbed out of the car.

"Yes," Mum said, now sounding exasperated, "but in all my years with horses I've never seen one that difficult. You need to stop thinking with your heart, Vicki, and think with your head. Buying Casper just doesn't add up. With Dandy you're already winning Champions and jumping to 95 centimetres. If you get another pony, it should be one that's capable of doing more with you, not less. Casper will never be the type of pony to make any of your riding goals come true."

U U U

But Vicki wasn't going to let Casper go. The Arabian had crept his way into her heart. Every day that week, she hounded her parents in the hopes they would change their minds.

She tried bribery. "I'll do the dishes every night for a year," she said. When that didn't work, Kelly and Amanda helped her hide dozens of handwritten notes around the house for Mum and Dad to find, outlining all the reasons why they should let her save Casper. The first dozen she hid between plates in the kitchen cupboard; others she left under her parents' pillows and taped to food in the fridge.

Her dad laughed as he pulled a note off a bottle of milk he'd just opened at breakfast. *"I've always dreamed of owning an Arab, ever since I read* The Black Stallion. *Buying Casper would make that dream come true,"* he read out. "That hardly seems like a good reason to buy a troublesome pony. You're going to have to come up with something better than that, Vicki."

Vicki rolled her eyes. "No problem, I have plenty more where that came from!"

Shuffling through the pile of plates, she grabbed another note and read it out loud.

"*My instructor at Pony Club said it's the difficult ponies that have the most to teach us. I will learn a lot from training Casper and be a better horse-rider because of it.*"

Her parents looked at each other, momentarily lost for words. Vicki could see that this reason at least had impressed them, and crossed her fingers.

"You're like a broken record," Dad said at last, taking a sip of his coffee. "But we're not buying Casper. That's final."

"That pony needs me," Vicki said adamantly. She finished the last mouthful of her breakfast, and rose from the table. "I'm the only one who sees the potential in him."

Chapter 4
The Money Plan

ONE AFTERNOON, ON THEIR WAY home from school, rain pelted against the windows of the car and the window-wipers swished back and forth frantically. Wanting to delay getting saturated doing chores, Vicki rushed straight to her room and grabbed her piggy-bank. She'd talked over her pony problem with Stella during the lunch break and had come up with a great idea.

Shaking out the coins, she settled down and began counting. She'd been saving up for over a year now. If she could afford to buy Casper herself, surely then her parents would have to let her have him?

"Twenty-six dollars," Vicki whispered as she jotted down a simple maths equation. "That means I still need another . . . two hundred and twenty-four."

She racked her brain thinking of ways to earn more money, and soon had a very short list.

How can I make enough money to buy Casper?
- Sell horse manure — $4 per sack
- Pull weeds out of the paddocks — $1 per sack

As Vicki stared at the sheet of paper, her sisters rushed into their little shared bedroom. She snatched up the list and hid it behind her back — but not quite fast enough.

"What are you hiding?" Kelly asked suspiciously.

"Nothing." Vicki avoided her sisters' gaze. "Just homework."

"Why have you emptied your piggy-bank?" Kelly asked, her eyes trained on the piled-up coins.

Defeated, Vicki sighed. "I was hoping I'd have

enough money to buy Casper, but I'm not even close."

Amanda perched on the edge of her bed, her eyes focused on her own piggy-bank on the windowsill. "You can borrow my money."

"Mine, too," Kelly offered. "I was saving up to buy a velvet helmet, but rescuing Casper is much more important."

Vicki smiled gratefully as they lifted their piggy-banks off the windowsill. The rain continued beating against the window-panes, almost drowning out the sound of her sisters emptying their piggy-banks onto the bed.

"I've saved thirty-one dollars," Kelly said proudly.

"How much do I have?" Amanda asked.

"You've got fourteen," Vicki said when she'd finished counting. "With all our pocket money together it's a big help, but I'll still need nearly a hundred and eighty dollars. I thought I might be able to sell sacks of horse manure or pull weeds to earn the rest of the money."

"That'll take ages," Amanda groaned, and began grabbing handfuls of coins and slotting them back into her piggy-bank.

Vicki sighed. She knew her little sister was right. They'd been pulling weeds and selling bags of manure for as long as they could remember, but between the three of them they'd only managed to save seventy-one dollars.

"I have an idea," Kelly said, suddenly sitting up. "If you buy the ribbons, I could make you some show browbands to sell."

Just a few months earlier Kelly had saved them all a lot of money by making each of their ponies — Cameo, Dandy and Charlie — show browbands for the Royal Easter Show. Her browbands looked so good nobody had known they were homemade.

"They sell in shops for one hundred dollars each, but even if we charged only half that amount, we'd be able to afford Casper in no time."

"Really? You'd do that for me?" Vicki asked. It took her sister a couple of hours to make each browband, so it would be much faster than any of her other ways to earn money.

"We could ask Dad to teach us how to make rope halters, too," Kelly said, her voice rising in excitement as she held out a hand for the pen and paper. "The one he made for Dandy when he was wild is even better than the ones from the horse shop."

Vicki watched as Kelly scribbled on the list, then passed it back for her to look at.

How can ~~I~~ we make enough money to buy Casper?
- Sell horse manure — $4 per sack
- Pull weeds out of the paddocks — $1 per sack
- Make and sell show browbands — $50 each
- Make and sell rope halters — $15 each

As she read over the list, Vicki felt the tension leaving her shoulders. Having enough money to save Casper suddenly seemed within her grasp.

"Now we just need to convince Mum and Dad," Vicki smiled, unable to contain her optimism. "Then head into town to buy ribbons and rope."

"Can I help pick the colours?" Amanda begged.

Ten minutes later, Vicki and her sisters were pulling on their gumboots, heading out on the farm in search of their parents. A storm was brewing, and the girls found them moving jumps and collecting buckets in case the river flooded. A quick glance showed it was already threatening to burst its banks.

"You girls need to get your ponies out of the back paddock," Dad yelled above the wind. "If the rain is as heavy as they're predicting, it'll be underwater by morning."

Forgetting about their plans to make money, Vicki and her sisters ran to the tack shed and grabbed halters. As they sloshed through the mud in search of their ponies, Amanda ran ahead, slipping and sliding in the puddles. Her laughter was contagious, and soon Vicki and Kelly joined in. By the time they reached their ponies, they looked like mud monsters, and Dandy took off at a canter when he saw them.

"You're a silly boy," Vicki said fondly. She wiped the mud from her face and followed after him. Soon she had Dandy caught, and the girls led him, Cameo and Charlie, along with their mother's pony, Jude, along the river's edge and up the hill to a more sheltered paddock.

After feeding all their animals, Vicki headed back to the house, careful to leave her muddy clothes in a pile by the door. She hurriedly showered and dressed in her pyjamas, then waited impatiently in the kitchen for the rest of the family.

At last, everyone was clean and dry, and while her mother cooked dinner, Vicki was finally able to broach the subject of their plan to save Casper.

"Kelly, Amanda and I have put together all our savings and we have seventy-one dollars," she began, twisting the tablecloth nervously in her hand. "If we can earn the rest of the money by ourselves, we were wondering if you'd let us buy Casper?"

Silence filled the room. As soon as she dared, Vicki looked up to see that Mum had stopped stirring the gravy, wooden spoon poised in mid-air as she made eye contact with her husband. Kelly and Amanda were hovering with eyes as big as saucers.

"It's a lot of money to raise," Mum said finally, and resumed stirring. "It'll take a lot of hard work."

"We've never been afraid of hard work," Vicki reminded her. "We've already made a plan for how we'll earn the money."

"I'm going to make browbands to sell," Kelly said

tentatively. "And we were wondering, Dad, if you'd teach us how to make rope halters as well."

Vicki glanced at her dad, and was relieved to see his expression softening. "I'd love to teach you how to make rope halters. You'll pick it up in no time and it will be a good money-earner."

As Vicki watched, her dad gave her mum a questioning look, and caught a barely perceivable nod. Hope filled her.

"Mum and I have been talking about it all week, and although we don't think buying Casper makes any sense, we actually admire your passion and determination—" Dad began.

"You *have* to let us buy Casper!" Amanda interrupted. "I'm giving Vicki all the money from my piggy-bank. I'd saved it up to buy a slingshot."

Holding up a hand, Dad quietened Amanda. "I wasn't finished," he said. "*If* you can raise the money, and *if* Casper hasn't sold by then, you can have him."

"Yesssss!" Vicki yelled, giving them both a hug. "You're the best parents in the world!"

"Don't get too excited," Mum warned. "Dad and I are hoping someone else will have bought him by then, so we don't have to!"

Chapter 5
The Final Dollars

THE NEXT COUPLE OF WEEKS passed slowly, even
though they were filled with chores. Every spare
minute the girls had was spent weeding the paddocks, picking up horse manure to sell and making
rope halters. Kelly also made a show browband for
one of their friends who wanted one.

"We've run out of weeds to pull, and we still have
sixty-seven dollars to earn," Vicki said one day as
they scoured the paddocks. Her shoulders stooped
when she saw only grass and clover remained. The
longer they took to earn the money, the more likely

that Casper would be sold — or worse.

"How about we see if you can give pony rides on Charlie and Cameo at the local market on Saturday?" their mum suggested at dinner that night. "Those two love children, and a morning's work won't hurt them."

Nodding eagerly, Vicki and her sisters waited as she made some phone calls.

"It's all sorted," Mum smiled at their expectant faces. "We have to have the ponies there by 7 a.m. and we can lead people around the car park."

"We better make some signs," Kelly said, and began collecting sheets of used cardboard and marker pens.

Soon Vicki had written out the signs, and Kelly and Amanda set about colouring in the letters. When they finished they sat back and admired their handiwork.

PONY RIDES,
$2 FOR 5 MINUTES

Vicki suddenly clapped a hand to her head. In her excitement, she'd forgotten that the ponies hadn't been ridden for the past month. "We'd better give Cameo and Charlie a ride first, to make sure they'll behave!"

∪ ∪ ∪

Saturday morning finally arrived, and Vicki rose some time before the sun. The days were now dawning much later, and she wanted to have everything perfectly ready. Hurrying outside, where her breath frosted in mid-air, she packed the signs and Charlie and Cameo's gear before catching her sister's ponies, removing their blankets and brushing them until their coats shone.

"I'm so lucky you two are quiet enough for strangers to ride," Vicki chatted to the ponies as she worked. "Dandy and Jude would never be patient enough for pony rides!"

At 6.30 a.m. her sisters appeared outside, bundled into coats and scarves and looking dishevelled and sleepy.

"Mum says it's time to load the ponies on the truck," Kelly yawned.

Twenty minutes later they had arrived at the market. Once Cameo and Charlie were saddled, Vicki carefully set up their handmade signs by the entrance, pointing people in the right direction.

Soon they had their first customers. Vicki carefully pocketed the coins, knowing that with each pony ride she was a couple of dollars closer to saving Casper. As she and Dad carefully led the ponies with their riders around the car park, little children started pointing at the ponies and pulling their parents over to join the growing line.

For the next three hours Cameo and Charlie walked around and around the car park tirelessly, and the pile of gold coins grew bigger and bigger.

Finally, the market came to an end and the stall owners began packing up their stands. Grabbing a gold coin, Vicki rushed over and bought Cameo and Charlie some carrots as a reward for being so patient and gentle with all of the kids.

When she returned, Kelly, Amanda and their mum were grinning like idiots.

"We made over a hundred dollars!" Amanda

cried. "Way more than you needed to buy Casper!"

Vicki froze, unable to believe it. Slowly she turned to her mum, her eyes questioning. Her mum nodded.

"As soon as we're home, you can ring up and see if he's still available."

Chapter 6
Home Sweet Home

AN HOUR LATER THEY WERE HOME. Once the ponies were back in their paddocks grazing, Vicki rushed into the house to call Casper's owner. With trembling fingers, she dialled the number.

"I'm calling about Casper," she began, as soon as the lady answered. "Is he still for sale?"

"Yes, he is," she replied.

Vicki breathed a sigh of relief. "My family came out and tried him three weeks ago."

"Were you the nice family with the three girls? I remember that Casper let you brush him."

"Yes, that's right. I'm Vicki. I've finally saved up enough to buy him. Would it be possible to pick him up this afternoon?"

"Really?" Casper's owner replied in shock. "What time? I'll have him caught and waiting."

"We can be there in half an hour, if it suits?" Vicki said, pretending not to notice that her parents were frantically shaking their heads.

Hanging up the phone, Vicki danced around the room with her sisters. "Casper's coming home!"

"It's a twenty-minute drive," Dad scolded her. "There's no way we'll have the truck ready to leave in ten minutes."

Vicki put her hands on her hips. "I've been waiting for this moment for weeks — I can't bear the thought of waiting even a minute longer."

Dad looked at his daughter's determined face for a moment, and then chuckled. "You'd better hurry then," he said. "Run down to the shed and grab a halter. We'll meet you at the truck."

Just as the owner had promised, Casper was tied up to the rail and waiting for them when they arrived. As soon as the truck stopped, Vicki jumped out and ran eagerly over to him.

"I told you I'd be back," she said, reaching out to pat his chiselled head. Casper's eyes glinted, and he flattened his ears in warning. Vicki ducked backwards to avoid being bitten. It wasn't the reunion she had dreamed of. "I guess we're not friends yet," she said ruefully.

"Give him time," Mum encouraged her.

Dad narrowed his eyes as he watched Casper. "He couldn't possibly get any worse, that's for sure. Let's get his halter changed then load up, so we can be home before dark."

Vicki changed Casper's halter carefully, quickly moving out of reach every time he swiped at her with his teeth. Fear flickered in her stomach as she realised there was a real chance that Casper could injure her.

"Come on, boy," Vicki whispered to the pony, as she led him over to the truck. "You'll like living with us."

To everyone's surprise, Casper leapt eagerly on

the truck and soon the ramp was closed.

"This is for you," Vicki said to his owner, as she passed over the money she and her sisters had saved. Suddenly it felt real. Casper was finally hers!

"Promise you'll be careful with him," the lady cautioned. "I'd feel awful if he hurt you."

"I will," Vicki promised her. "But I have a feeling he's going to be fine. We'll be friends in no time."

"For his sake, and yours, I really hope that's true. He deserves to be happy."

∪ ∪ ∪

For the entire drive home she wondered about Casper's future, trying to imagine what he'd be like a year from now. When she'd been taming Dandy, and training Cameo for Kelly, she'd been able to visualise them winning ribbons and jumping at competitions. But for Casper, the future looked cloudy.

Then, as they pulled into their driveway twenty minutes later, she suddenly saw it clearly: Casper trotting towards her with his ears pricked, standing contentedly while she scratched his neck. In that moment, she realised something. Casper didn't have to be a champion in the competition arena; in fact, he didn't even have to be ridden if it was something he hated.

"I just want you to enjoy life," Vicki told Casper as she led him down the ramp, keeping the rope short so he couldn't pull away from her. Casper didn't seem reassured by this, however. Waving his head wildly, he looked around at his new surroundings. When he saw the other ponies in the front paddock, he neighed out desperately, fighting against Vicki as he tried to join them.

"Where are we putting him?" Vicki asked her mum, tightening her grip on the rope.

Mum thought quickly and turned to her second daughter. "Kelly, why don't you run down and catch Cameo and we'll introduce them to each other. Your pony is so calm and steady, and if they get along, Casper might be more relaxed grazing with another pony."

"He won't have seen another pony in almost a year," Vicki realised. "Oh Casper, how lonely for you."

When Kelly approached with Cameo, Vicki kept a close eye on her new pony, who was tugging on his lead and trying to inch closer to the placid, steel-grey mare. The ponies reached out their heads to say hello to each other.

"Just be careful they don't kick each other, or strike out and get you with a front hoof," Mum cautioned. But instead, Casper nickered softly and nudged Cameo repeatedly. Cameo seemed less than impressed, but patiently tolerated the new arrival's attention.

"I think they're going to be fine," Mum said to Vicki in relief. "Let's leave the two of them together. If they're settled by tomorrow then Charlie, Dandy and Jude can join them."

Chapter 7
Less is More

ALTHOUGH IT WAS A STRUGGLE, Vicki managed to leave Casper alone for a few days so he could settle in. It was hardest the day after Casper's arrival, since it was Sunday and there was no school to distract her. For hours she leant on the railing watching Casper graze, and when that grew boring she caught Dandy and groomed him.

As she brushed Dandy's coat, she reminded herself that he hadn't always been trusty and reliable. At the beginning he'd been unpredictable and difficult, just like Casper, and Vicki was confident that, with time, her grey Arabian would settle down, too.

Every evening when the girls came out to feed the ponies, Casper would hang back, but gradually he started to walk up and eat some hay while Vicki and her sisters stood nearby patting the other ponies.

"I haven't seen your ears go back since you arrived," Vicki told Casper on their fifth evening together. "Maybe tomorrow I'll try to catch you."

The next day, when the girls got home from school, the family gathered at the paddock gate. Slowly Vicki approached the new pony, stopping to pat Dandy on her way. Casper watched her curiously, his ears flicking.

As soon as she lifted the halter, he bared his teeth and reared. Vicki paused, fear racing through her. "It's all right, boy," she said. "I don't have to catch you today. How about I just give you a pat?"

Dropping the halter, Vicki stepped closer, relieved that Casper seemed calmer. Dandy, Cameo and Charlie crowded around her, wanting more attention, and slowly Casper stepped forward to join them. But as she laid a hand on the Arabian's neck, he swung his head uneasily.

"As soon as you relax, I'll leave," Vicki promised

him, as she slowly stroked his neck. Over the next few minutes she felt the tension leave Casper's body, and when she saw the fire leaving his eyes, Vicki lowered her hand and backed away.

"See, that wasn't so hard, was it?" she whispered, turning to join the rest of her family at the fence.

For the next week, Vicki continued working with Casper every afternoon after she got home from school. She no longer took the halter out with her, but instead just spent a few minutes with him each time she checked or fed the ponies. Day by day, Casper got a little easier to approach and stayed relaxed for longer while she patted him.

"Will you freak out if I go and get the halter?" Vicki asked Casper as she stroked his neck.

Vicki was filled with nervous anticipation as she returned with the halter. She was sure Casper was starting to trust her and didn't want him to turn nasty on her again.

"See, it's not so bad," Vicki said, as she reached

out and laid a hand on Casper's neck. Slowly she lifted the halter off her shoulder, but the movement startled the pony and he backed away. He stamped a hoof, and although he didn't rear he flattened his ears and watched her warily. For five minutes they faced each other in a stand-off.

"I just need you to flick an ear forward," Vicki told Casper, "or sigh, or lick your lips, or step forward. You can even shake your head. Anything to show me that you're relaxing."

Patiently Vicki waited, her eyes never leaving Casper's. The timing was crucial and she knew, from working with Dandy when he was a wild pony just off the mountain, how important it was to understand and respond to Casper's body language.

And then it happened: Casper exhaled and lowered his head for just a fraction of a second. Vicki rewarded him by backing away a few steps, to give him space.

"That was a pretty big deal for you, huh?" she smiled proudly. "But you didn't rear, or show me your teeth, so I'm happy."

Again she approached Casper, watching him closely. In the instant he tensed, before he could react badly, Vicki stopped her advance and stood quietly watching him. This time it only took a few minutes for Casper to chew his lips and relax, and Vicki was quick to retreat again.

For the next half an hour they danced, forward and backwards. At last she stood in front of Casper, who let her secure the halter on his head.

"That was amazing," Vicki whispered to the relaxed pony. "It might have been slow, but there wasn't any bad behaviour!"

Stepping away, she led Casper around the paddock and was amused when she saw Cameo, who was always keen to play follow-the-leader, fall into line behind him. Once they completed the circle, she took the halter off and set Casper free. She watched as he wandered over to join his new friends. "You sure are happier with the other ponies for company, aren't you, boy?"

Vicki turned and headed for the gate with a spring in her step. Glancing back, she saw that Casper was watching her and a smile of pure happiness broke over her face.

Chapter 8
Bareback Pony

THE NEXT DAY IT ONLY TOOK ten minutes to halter Casper, and Vicki was lightheaded with joy. He was making progress!

Within a week, Vicki could catch Casper like a normal pony, and each day she'd lead him out on an adventure. There were a number of times, as they ventured around their property or down the roads, that Vicki thought he was almost ready to ride. But not wanting to rush things, she waited patiently for the right moment.

"I think today's the day," Vicki told Casper as

she finished brushing him one morning. Casper was more relaxed than ever, and had stood dozing while Vicki brushed every inch of his body and picked out all four of his hooves.

Heading for the tack shed, she collected her saddle and bridle and made her way back to the tie-up rails. Carefully she laid the saddle across Casper's back. He moved restlessly in response.

Vicki reached for the girth, but paused when Casper pinned his ears back, talking quietly to reassure him. "Woah, boy, I promise it's not as awful as you think."

Slowly she tightened the girth on the saddle, then put a bridle on over his halter. Although Casper didn't misbehave, from the way he chomped on the bit and pinned his ears back it was obvious he was unhappy. Vicki felt terrible.

As she led him off, Casper dragged on the rope, something he hadn't done since they'd first seen him. Hoping he'd get used to the feel of the gear, Vicki clipped the lead onto Casper's bit and asked him to trot in a big circle around her. Disappointment filled her when she pulled on the rope to slow him and he reared up.

Vicki sighed. "This just isn't working, is it?" Casper had seemed so contented over the past few days, but with the saddle and bridle on, he was back to his old ways. Stroking Casper's head, she wondered what to do next. Casper nuzzled her, then swung his head to look back at the saddle, chomping on the bit.

"The saddle and bridle have to go," Vicki said as she looked at her unhappy pony. "Is that what you're trying to tell me?"

Vicki untacked Casper and laid the saddle and bridle over the gate. Instantly, Casper's mood lifted and he pricked his ears forward.

"Maybe you're a bareback pony?" Vicki wondered as she studied the highly strung Arabian. "I think we need to start from scratch and train you with just a halter on, the same way we started Dandy and Cameo."

She tied Casper up, and sprinted back to the tack shed to grab her helmet. Then she went in search of her mum and dad. It was a family rule that her parents had to be there if the girls were trying something new with their ponies, just in case something went wrong.

"I'm going to ride Casper for the first time," Vicki

told her sisters as she ran past them on the lawn, where they were playing with their pets. "Meet in the front paddock in a few minutes?"

Not wanting to miss out on the action, Amanda quickly put her rat back in his cage, and Kelly lifted the rabbits into their hutch. Once all of the animals were safely away, they joined Vicki and their parents at the fence.

"He's been ridden before, right?" Amanda asked her mum as she climbed up and sat on the gate.

"Yes, but only a handful of times in the past year, and he's been difficult every time."

Excited and nervous at the same time, Vicki turned to Casper, who stood waiting patiently. If everything went as well as she hoped, she'd be riding him in no time at all.

Gently, she jumped up and lay over his bare back, as if she was mounting an unbroken pony for the very first time. Casper showed no concern as she lay there, so, after a few minutes, she moved to sitting upright on his back.

"He certainly seems relaxed at the moment," Dad said, impressed. "You sure do have a gift with horses."

Vicki smiled, glad everyone else was starting to see how special Casper was, too. At Vicki's urging, he stepped out eagerly around the paddock.

"How about a trot?" Vicki asked the pony as she squeezed with her heels. Casper quietly broke into a trot, more relaxed than he'd ever been, and Vicki grinned.

But with each stride, her grin faded into a frown. Casper might be behaving perfectly, but he was the most uncomfortable pony to ride bareback!

"He's so bouncy at the trot," Vicki complained as she brought him back to a halt in front of her family. "And his wither is so bony."

"Perhaps he'll be easier to sit on once he's gained some weight," Mum replied. "He is still quite skinny."

"Try a canter," Kelly suggested. "That should be smoother."

This time Vicki let Casper trot for only a few strides before encouraging him into a canter. His long mane whipped her face as they circled the paddock, and he remained steady beneath her. Laughing, she slowed Casper to a stop, wrapping her arms around her pony's neck.

"Never in a million years did I imagine I'd be

cantering you when I woke up this morning," she whispered into his ear.

As if in understanding, Casper tossed his head. Vicki leapt to the ground, and gave him another hug before undoing his halter and setting him loose.

"I knew you had potential, Casper, but I never dreamed you would be this good so soon!"

Chapter 9
Taking a Tumble

THE NEXT FEW DAYS Vicki felt like she was in a dream: every day she rode the Arabian bareback with a halter, and Casper didn't put a foot wrong. Encouraged by his good behaviour, she decided it was time to ride him out on the neighbour's farm. Her sisters would be bringing along their ponies, so Casper would have some company.

"It feels so good to be on Cameo again," Kelly sighed happily. "I've missed riding her so much."

"Charlie's going to enjoy himself, too," Amanda agreed, as she clambered onto her little pony's back.

"I know the holiday was good for him, so he could rest after the Royal Easter Show, but I think he was starting to get bored in the paddock."

Vicki tuned out their chatter as she slipped a bridle on Casper in case she needed extra control while out riding on the farm. Although he was a little unsure, he didn't seem nearly as anxious as the first time. She smiled hopefully. Maybe, now that he'd had a few good rides and trust had built up between them, all his other issues would improve.

Vaulting onto his bare back, she followed her sisters down the road, heading towards the farm. But right from the start Casper was unsettled. Vicki had to keep a firm grip with her legs as he jumped sideways passing the letterbox. Even the white lines on the road seemed to scare him. It took all of Vicki's focus to stay balanced.

"He's not having a good day, is he?" Kelly said, looking over in concern. She sat relaxed on steady Cameo, who was completely at home riding on the road. "I'm glad I'm not the one riding him. Maybe we should head back?"

Vicki shook her head. "Let's keep going. I think he's just scared of all the new sights, but once we reach the farm gate there won't be as much to spook him. Remember, he hadn't left his own property for more than a year before he came to us, and so far I've only ridden him in the front paddock."

Soon they turned off the road into the neighbour's driveway. As they neared the farm gate, Vicki pulled back on the reins, asking Casper to halt. The Arabian sharply threw his head in the air and spun around, causing Vicki to slip sideways. Clutching the reins to regain her balance, she hung on desperately as Casper reared. But she was already dislodged, and she tumbled to the ground, rolling to the side to avoid Casper's flailing hooves.

"Are you all right?" Amanda asked, jumping off Charlie and running over to Vicki. "You hit the ground hard!"

It had been a long time since she'd taken a fall off a pony. Vicki stiffly rose to her feet, not quite sure what had happened. "I think so," she grimaced. She poked her hip, which felt as if it was already starting to bruise.

Looking around, she saw Casper grazing on a clump of grass by the gate, and limped over to him. "What was that for?" Vicki asked her pony in confusion. "You've been doing so well."

She led him through the gate on foot, then leapt back on, knowing she needed to ride him again straight away so he wouldn't learn any bad habits.

"Let's just walk up this hill," Vicki told her sisters as she settled on his back. "I'd rather not risk falling off again."

Casper seemed calm and relaxed as they made their way up the hill. Vicki's confidence was returning, so she took the lead, cantering him up the next slope. But as she reached the top and slowed him back to a trot, Casper tossed his head violently and bucked. Vicki grabbed for a handful of mane to stop herself slipping off, but it was too late. She threw herself to the side, landing on her feet before falling forward onto her knees.

"I think you should lead him home," Kelly pleaded with her sister, bringing Cameo to a halt, with Amanda and Charlie following suit. "He's not safe."

"Most of the time he's perfect," Vicki said in frustration, shaking her hair out of her eyes. "It makes no sense."

Her entire body now felt battered and bruised, but she knew that if Casper didn't finish on a good note she'd be worried about riding him the next day. Catching him again, she hesitantly remounted.

"Let's head back," she said. The sisters turned their ponies towards home, walking the entire way.

Chapter 10
Slow Progress

BACK AT HOME, just as they reached the tie-up rail, Vicki pulled on the reins, asking Casper to halt. But once again he reared.

Struggling to stay on, Vicki clung to his mane and gripped tightly with her legs. Several seconds passed as if in slow motion, as Casper balanced precariously on his hind legs. When he finally dropped back onto all four legs again, Vicki leapt to the ground, shaken.

"He's been so well behaved the past few days," Vicki said as she unbridled him. "There has to be something causing him to act badly."

"Maybe he doesn't like open spaces?" Amanda suggested.

"Or it could be the bridle," Kelly added. "He was fine in the halter."

Vicki swung around and stared at her sister, her mind connecting the dots.

"You're right! It's every time we slow down," she exclaimed.

"What are you talking about?" Amanda asked.

"Casper only reacts badly when I'm pulling on the reins!" Vicki explained, with growing excitement. "The first and the last times he reared were when I was asking him to halt, and the second time he bucked when I was asking him to slow from a canter to a trot."

"So how are you going to fix that?" Kelly said, frowning. "You know you can't just ride Casper at one speed."

"No, don't you get it?" Vicki said. All the pieces were clicking into place. "It must be the bit. He doesn't like it."

Kelly gasped as she understood. "That actually makes sense! Let's try riding out on the farm again tomorrow, and this time you can try him in a halter instead of the bridle."

Although Vicki was stiff and sore the next morning, nothing could stop her from feeling positive. Now that she had decided the bit was to blame, with Casper back in a halter she was confident the ride would go smoothly.

But when the girls retraced their steps from the day before, as soon as Casper was out on the road he spooked in all the same places. Vicki was filled with dismay.

"Maybe I was wrong about the bit," Vicki cried as she fought to stay on her anxious pony. "So far he's exactly the same."

"I read once that Arabians are more sensitive than other breeds," Kelly said, reassuringly. "Let's just see how he goes once we're off the road."

When they reached the gate where Vicki had fallen off the day before, she braced herself and asked Casper to stop. Relief flooded her when he calmly came back to a halt.

"So far, so good," Amanda smiled, as she jumped off to open the gate.

To test him, the girls cantered up the hill, and again Casper behaved well. In fact, he seemed the happiest Vicki had ever seen him. From paddock to paddock they ventured, stopping and turning as often as possible, and not once did Casper misbehave.

"So most of his issues do come from wearing the bridle and the saddle," Vicki mused, as they rode home. "I wonder what's happened to him in the past to make him hate being ridden with gear on?"

"If you can only ride him bareback and in a halter, you'll never be able to ride him at Pony Club or at competitions," Kelly pointed out. "What are you going to do with him?"

"I'm not sure," Vicki said. "I just have to keep hoping that he'll get used to them over time."

∪ ∪ ∪

But Vicki soon learnt that time made no difference. As the season changed from winter to spring, Casper was no better or worse. If she rode him bareback with a halter he was faultless, but every time she tried him with a saddle and bridle it always ended badly.

Put off by falling so many times, she eventually stopped trying to ride him with gear on. It seemed as though her mum had been right all along — Casper would never be a show pony. But Vicki wasn't going to let that get her down.

"Luckily I'm good at riding without a saddle," she whispered to Casper one cold, clear Saturday morning. "If you're not going to let me ride you with gear on, then I guess we'll just do everything bareback. First, let's see if you can jump."

She led him down to the jumping paddock, where she had set up two small crossbars. Her sisters were ready and waiting with Charlie and Cameo all saddled and bridled, and as soon as Vicki was astride Casper they began to warm up their ponies.

After several minutes, Vicki gave the signal. Amanda and Kelly turned their mounts to canter into the jumps, with Vicki following close behind.

Just as Vicki had hoped, Casper cleared them effortlessly and kept a smooth rhythm that made riding bareback bearable. Elated, she patted his neck before dismounting and raising the fences higher.

"You really are remarkable," she told her pony once they cleared a jump set at 70 centimetres. "I'm pretty sure you've been taught to jump before."

Every day, Vicki spent time with each of her ponies, training them over the jumps. Within a few weeks, she could jump Casper to the same height as Dandy. The first show of the season was only a month away, and Dandy was training well. Vicki was looking forward to competing on her beautiful chestnut, and the only disappointment was that, because Casper wouldn't wear a saddle or bridle, he wouldn't be able to join her and Dandy at events.

But Vicki was not about to let her beautiful Arabian go unappreciated and she started thinking of ways to show him off to her friends.

Chapter 11
Sleepover Shenanigans

"I THINK WE SHOULD INVITE a couple of friends who have ponies to a sleepover this weekend," Vicki said to her sisters one evening in late September, as she put Casper away. Their training had gone particularly well that day — they'd jumped over a 1-metre oxer effortlessly. "Then the next day we can hold a jumping day and Casper can compete."

"Good thinking," Kelly said. "We should invite Annabelle, since she lives just up the hill."

"The more the merrier," Vicki smiled. "I'm sure

Stella will come, too. She's always asking at school how Casper is going, plus we can all meet her new pony, Diego."

After months of searching, Stella had finally fallen in love with a pretty bay gelding who'd had lots of success in Pony Club competitions. She'd bought him just a couple of weeks earlier.

But Mum wasn't so sure when they told her their plan. "Where will everyone sleep?" she asked.

Vicki glanced at her sisters, all of a sudden unsure. Their house was very small — the three sisters all shared a bedroom as it was. "What about in the truck or tack shed? Or if the weather's good we could even sleep under the stars."

"With a camp fire and everything!" Amanda said, catching on to the idea.

"Camping out will be a real adventure," Kelly grinned.

"And what are you going to do for meals while camping?" Mum asked.

Again, the girls looked at each other. They hadn't thought that far ahead. Feeding two extra kids and their ponies for a weekend would also be extra work for their parents.

"Everyone could bring a little bit of money," Vicki said, thinking fast. "And on the first day we'll ride down to the supermarket on our ponies and buy food to cook over the camp fire."

"Sounds like you've thought of everything," Mum said, giving in with a smile. "Send out the invites."

∪ ∪ ∪

"Everyone ready?" Vicki asked as she mounted Dandy. Around her, a chorus of "yes" filled the air. It was a beautiful but cold spring morning, without a cloud in the sky.

Vicki zipped up her jacket to keep warm, and checked her pocket for her five-dollar note before riding to the front of the group. Their first mission was to buy food, just like they'd promised Mum.

Over in the paddock, Casper watched Vicki forlornly. He looked as if he was wondering why he was being left behind.

"We're off to the supermarket," Vicki called out to him as they rode away. "There's no way I'd feel safe riding you down the main roads, since you still spook at everything."

Leading the way, Vicki glanced back at the trail of riders behind her. Their friends had leapt at the chance to stay for the weekend, especially as it involved camping out together. Annabelle had her pony, Blackie, and Stella looked very happy on Diego.

In single file they made their way up a small side street, before turning their ponies onto the main road towards town. They had been riding for about ten minutes when Amanda spoke up from the back of the group.

"Do you think Charlie suits his new look?"

Turning, Vicki looked over her shoulder at Amanda and couldn't help but laugh. She had flowers of every colour poking out from her helmet, and Charlie had even more twisted into his bridle and mane.

"You look ridiculous!" she laughed.

"Ridiculously awesome!" Amanda grinned, plucking another flower from a tree as she passed.

The girls dismounted in the car park by the store. Gathering five dollars from each person, Vicki then divided the money in half and split the girls into two groups.

"We'll go in turns," Vicki explained. "My group will stay and hold the ponies while the others buy food for breakfast and lunch for tomorrow, then we'll swap. We'll be in charge of buying dinner tonight."

Vicki, Annabelle and Amanda stayed with the ponies first, while the others shopped. Within seconds, two kids approached with their parents.

"Do you mind if we pat your ponies?" one asked.

"Not at all," Amanda said, leading Charlie and Cameo forward for the kids to pat. "These two are the friendliest."

Soon there was a line of people wanting to meet the horses, and one by one they stepped forward to say hello.

When the others rejoined them, armed with only a single bag of food, Vicki glanced at her watch, amazed to see that more than ten minutes had passed.

"Fifteen dollars is nowhere near enough money to buy food for five people," Kelly declared, as she showed the others the contents of the shopping bag.

Amanda leaned over to have a peek. "Yum!" she said in delight.

Vicki looked inside and gasped in shock. The

girls had bought only apples, chocolate-chip cookies and marshmallows to cook over the camp fire. "This is snack food! What are we going to eat for lunch?"

"We couldn't afford anything else," Stella said, with a shamefaced shrug.

"I guess it's our turn," Vicki said, passing over the ponies' reins. "Hopefully we can do a little better!"

Dashing through the store, with the flowers on Amanda's helmet bobbing, Vicki took charge. "Let's buy food we can actually make over a camp fire."

"What about spaghetti for breakfast?" Annabelle suggested. "When we camp out at our farm we put the cans in the embers of the fire to warm up."

"Great idea," Vicki said, as they filled their shopping basket. "We can also cook potatoes wrapped in tinfoil for dinner tonight."

∪ ∪ ∪

That evening, with the ponies safely in their paddocks, Vicki sat with her sisters and their friends around the camp fire, eating a charred potato out of her grubby hands. Food had never tasted so good.

"We're going to freeze tonight," Stella groaned, as she pulled on an extra layer of clothing. "Maybe we should be staying in the tack shed, or the horse truck."

"You're such a city girl," Vicki teased. "It's time you learnt to rough it like the rest of us country kids."

"Hey, it's not my fault I grew up in town!"

"No, it's not," Annabelle laughed. "But if you wimp out on us and sleep somewhere else we're going to give you grief!"

"Oh, all right," Stella said, throwing her hands in the air. "I'll sleep under the stars. It will be a once in a lifetime experience, that's for sure."

They had all decided that sleeping outdoors was a great idea a few hours earlier, in the bright afternoon sunshine. Before darkness closed in, they set up their beds.

First the girls spread out an old tarpaulin so their bedding wouldn't get wet from the damp grass, then they piled on their blankets, and laid old horse covers on top for extra warmth. Once it was dark, they snuggled under the covers, telling stories and laughing. Gradually their voices became more muted as tiredness took over.

As she listened to the others talking, Vicki gazed up into the starry night sky, searching for shooting stars.

She jolted upright, suddenly wide awake. "Anyone keen for a moonlit farm ride?"

"Me!" Amanda said, sitting up. "Charlie will love it, even if it is way past my bed-time."

"Is it safe?" Stella asked uncertainly. "Can horses even see in the dark?"

"Of course they can," Kelly said, with a roll of her

eyes. "Do we need to let Mum and Dad know?"

"They'll be asleep by now," Vicki said. "I think we'll be okay if we don't go too far."

"I've never ridden in the dark before," Annabelle said, as she quickly pulled on her riding boots. "But I bet it'll be lots of fun!"

Chapter 12
Moonlight Madness

AT THE TACK SHED, EVERYONE grabbed their helmets and bridles, deciding it would be too complicated to saddle up in the dark. Vicki was the last one to leave, her hand hovering first over Dandy's bridle and then Casper's halter. Finally, she stretched forward and snatched the halter off the wall, hoping she wasn't making a mistake by riding the less-experienced pony on their midnight adventure.

Running up the hill, she headed for Casper's paddock, slowing when she saw Kelly and Amanda had already caught their ponies and were leading them down the driveway towards her.

"You're riding Casper?" Kelly gasped when she saw her sister emerge out of the darkness. "I figured you'd take Dandy."

"I've already ridden him today," Vicki said with a shrug. Behind them, she saw that Casper was waiting for her at the gate. "Besides, I think Casper would wonder why he was being left behind for the second time in one day."

"Good luck catching him in the dark," Amanda yawned, as she ambled down the hill with Charlie. "Don't keep us waiting too long."

Vicki approached Casper, talking softly.

"Everyone else is ready to go, so here's the deal. If you'll let me catch you in under two minutes I'll ride you. Otherwise I'll take Dandy instead."

Slipping through the gate, Vicki reached out a hand towards Casper. Tossing his head, he sidestepped and turned back in the direction in which the other ponies had disappeared, letting out a shrill neigh.

"You're OK, boy," Vicki reassured him as she laid a hand on his trembling shoulder. "I know it's scary in the dark, but I promise I'm still the same person that I am in the daylight. We trust each other, right?"

Slowly she felt him relax, and when the tremors stopped she reached up and haltered him. Opening the gate, she hurried to join the others.

"Sorry to keep you waiting," Vicki apologised as she swung up onto Casper's back. "He only took a little convincing before he remembered we were friends."

"That's OK," Stella's voice rang through the gloom. "I've been waiting months to watch you ride him, and now I can hardly see him in the dark. He's just a blur of white, like a ghost in the night."

"I'll ride him again tomorrow," Vicki said. "He's changed a lot since you tried him!"

"He must have, if you trust him enough to ride him bareback in the dark," Stella replied, edging Diego closer to get a better look.

"You ride him in a halter?" asked Annabelle, who had ridden up on Vicki's other side. "How quiet is he?"

"He goes better like this," Vicki explained, as they started walking side by side on their ponies. "For some reason he hates the bridle — every time I put any contact on the bit he rears or bucks."

"Weird. If he behaved like that, I'd probably be too scared to ever ride him again, yet here you are with almost no gear on to control him. You're too brave for your own good."

"Without gear on to upset him, he's perfectly behaved," Vicki said, her voice filled with affection for her troublesome pony. "He's the most sensitive pony I've ever met."

"He sounds high-maintenance to me," Stella groaned. They picked up a trot as they reached the first hill on the farm. "I am so glad I didn't buy him!"

Vicki gripped her legs around Casper's sides to avoid the bouncing of his gait, but even then it was difficult to sit comfortably with his high-stepping Arabian trot. Squeezing her legs, Vicki urged Casper faster, letting out a sigh of relief when his rough gait evened out to a smooth canter.

∪ ∪ ∪

With only moonlight to guide them, the rest of Vicki's senses were enhanced as they flew up the hill. Her ears were filled with the rhythmic pounding of hooves, and against her legs she could feel Casper's steady heartbeat. His mane whipped her face as she leaned forward over his wither, and with another burst of speed she drew ahead of the other ponies. Closing her eyes, Vicki dropped the reins and spread her arms wide, caught up in the thrilling feeling of flying.

Drawing Casper to a halt at the top of the hill, Vicki waited for the others to catch up, her eyes struggling to make out who the shapes were in the dark.

"We better head back — our ponies are getting hot," Vicki said, laying her hand against Casper's steaming neck, her own breath freezing in the cool night air. "We're going to have to walk the entire way, so they have plenty of time to cool off."

"Can't we keep going?" Amanda asked, as she came to a halt on Charlie. "This is one of my favourite rides ever! In the dark I can pretend Charlie's as big as everyone else's pony!"

"Just one more hill," Annabelle pleaded. "Please!"

Vicki chewed on her lip. "I guess one more won't hurt," she finally conceded. "Why don't you guys walk to the bottom of this hill and canter up again? But I'll wait here — Casper's not as fit as your ponies."

"I'll stay with you," Kelly offered. "I think Cameo has had enough for tonight."

While the others headed back down the hill, Vicki and Kelly walked their ponies in circles to cool them off, planning out the jumping course for the following day.

"We'll need about ten jumps, but we only have two sets of jump standards and poles," Kelly worried.

"When's that ever stopped us?" Vicki laughed. "I'm sure we can make some jumps out of odds and ends."

Beneath her, Vicki felt Casper tense. Falling silent, she heard the sound of hooves approaching. Although they couldn't see the ponies yet, Casper had obviously heard them.

"That was the best feeling ever!" Annabelle cried out as she and Blackie emerged from the darkness, along with Stella and Diego.

Several seconds passed before Charlie also appeared, his little legs straining to catch up. Even in the semi-darkness it was impossible to miss the steam rising from his coat as he struggled to get his breath.

"Charlie's exhausted," Amanda said ruefully. "He could barely keep up."

"Casper's the same," Vicki said. "I think it's from the cold — there might be a frost in the morning. Let's get these ponies back home for some rest. I'm ready to sleep now, too!"

Chapter 13
Colic Crisis

VICKI WOKE AT DAWN. SITTING upright, she gazed in wonder at the icy world around her. A heavy frost coated the ground. Glancing up the hill, her eyes searched the paddocks to check on the ponies, and a soft smile lit her face as she saw Dandy, then Casper. She sighted Cameo and Jude, then Charlie — but as she watched the little grey, dread filled her.

He was swinging his head around and nipping at his stomach. Vicki knew it could only mean one thing: colic.

Fear filled her as memories of her earliest pony,

Bella, flashed to mind. Vicki remembered her feeling of hopelessness when Bella had fallen ill and the vets could do nothing to ease her pain, then the eventual heartbreak when the pony had been put to sleep.

Shaking everyone awake, she said urgently, "Kelly and Amanda, I need you to get Mum and Dad, then meet us at Charlie's paddock."

Vicki grabbed a halter and sprinted towards the paddock, not even taking the time to pull on her boots. Her friends followed closely behind. By the time they reached Charlie, Vicki's feet were numb, but she was so distracted by the sick pony she barely noticed.

"It's alright, Charlie Brown, we're here to help you," Vicki said, as she caught Charlie. She tried to sound firm, but her voice broke a little as she spoke.

Behind her she heard more voices as her parents ran across the paddock, Kelly and Amanda not far behind.

"Has he rolled?" Mum asked breathlessly.

"I don't know," Vicki said. "We took them for a moonlit ride on the farm last night—"

"You did *what*?"

"He was fine when I let him go," Amanda said, her eyes round and rapidly filling with tears. "He headed straight to the trough for a big drink."

"Cold water after a big ride isn't good," Annabelle murmured in concern. "My stepdad's a vet. We could call him since he's just up the road. He won't mind being woken."

"Is he going to be OK?" Amanda whispered as she hugged her pony's neck tightly.

"I hope so," Mum said, "but I can't make any promises." Placing a hand on Vicki's shoulder, she said, "I don't need to tell you how serious this is. Just make sure he doesn't roll while we go back to the house to get hold of Annabelle's dad."

Amanda's lip quivered. "Why can't he roll?"

"He might twist his intestines, which could cause a blockage," Vicki said, deliberately not mentioning how serious — or even fatal — that could be.

As they waited, Vicki walked Charlie in big circles, her heart breaking when she saw Amanda's huddled form by the fence. Kelly and Stella were trying to console her. Her sisters had been too young to remember losing Bella, but although several years had passed, Vicki would never forget just how devastating colic could be. Every time Charlie stopped to paw the ground or swing his head to his flanks, Vicki's breath caught.

"No one's answering the phone," Annabelle said breathlessly when she rejoined them a few minutes later. "They're probably still asleep."

Mum and Dad weren't far behind.

"Vicki, you and Annabelle need to ride up the hill to Annabelle's and get help. Dad and I would prefer to stay here to watch Charlie, and it'll be just as fast on horseback."

Vicki passed Charlie's rope to her mum.

"You can ride Cameo — it'll be faster than getting Blackie from the far paddock," Vicki said to Annabelle as she handed her the halter that was hanging over the gate along with a lead rope. She was about to head to the tack shed to get another halter when a cry stopped her.

"Hurry, girls! Charlie's down!"

Vicki's heart lurched when she saw Charlie lying on the ground, groaning. She grabbed the lead rope, sprinted for Casper and twisted it around his muzzle as a makeshift halter. Grabbing a handful of mane, she swung up onto his back and urged him forward, hoping she'd have enough control to guide him.

Dad held the gate open for them.

"Ride as fast as you can — Charlie needs help urgently," he said.

"Annabelle, you lead the way," Vicki urged as they trotted down the driveway and headed for the road, cantering on every grass verge to make up time. To Vicki's relief, Casper was following behind Cameo eagerly, responding to commands just as if he were wearing a halter.

A few minutes later, they turned into Annabelle's driveway. She tossed Cameo's reins to Vicki and ran into the house.

Her sleepy stepfather, Mike, soon emerged at the door, with Annabelle in tow. In his arms was a collection of vet supplies.

"I'll drive down and check Charlie now. You two can take your time riding back. It'll give your ponies time to cool off properly," Mike reassured them as he piled everything into his car and sped off down the driveway.

"Well, we'd better do as he said and walk the whole way home," Vicki said. Although she was worried about Charlie and impatient to get back, she knew it wouldn't help to risk their other ponies' health. "I hope Mike can help Charlie."

"Me too," Annabelle said.

◡ ◡ ◡

By the time Vicki and Annabelle returned, Mike had already treated Charlie. The little pony had been rugged up with a horse blanket to keep him warm, and now stood quietly beside Amanda.

"I think he's going to be OK. He's very lucky that he only has a mild case of colic and you caught him before he rolled," Mike said. He was holding a stethoscope against Charlie's gut, checking that it was making all the normal sounds. "Keep him close to the house so you can keep an eye on him over the next couple of hours, and call me if you're worried."

"Thanks for helping him," Amanda whispered tearfully as she stroked her pony's mane. "But I still don't understand — what made him get sick?"

"Colic is like a tummy ache for horses, and it can happen for lots of reasons," Mike explained. "But in Charlie's case, the cause was most likely too much cold water on a cold night, after getting hot and sweaty cantering up hills."

"So we shouldn't have ridden them in the dark?" Vicki questioned. She was feeling terribly guilty for having suggested the night ride.

"No, that was totally fine. But next time, make sure you walk them to cool them off for much longer than after a normal ride, especially if there's a chill in the air. And let them drink only a little bit of water at a time until their body temperature is back to normal."

Chapter 14
Odds and Ends

REASSURED THAT CHARLIE WAS making a good recovery, Mike drove away with a promise to come back later in the day.

Vicki was expecting to be told off for the night ride, but Mum and Dad, seeming to understand that watching Charlie suffer had been bad enough, simply suggested that they all have their breakfast.

The sun was by now high in the sky and the girls realised how hungry they were. They heated up their spaghetti in the embers of the fire and then, determined to carry on with their plans as best they could, set to work putting together a jumping course. First, they carried the sisters' jump stands and poles out of the river paddock and set them up on the lawn.

"Nice show jumps!" Annabelle said when she saw them. "At our farm we just have logs and old tyres to jump over."

"They're amazing, aren't they?" Vicki grinned. "Our grandad and Uncle Simon helped our dad make them for us last year!"

"But we don't have enough for a full course," Kelly explained, "so our next mission is to find random objects around the property to make about eight more jumps."

"What about those chairs?" Amanda asked, pointing towards the front porch. She was sitting on the grass, keeping a careful eye on Charlie, who seemed almost back to his normal self and was greedily snatching mouthfuls of grass.

"Great idea," Vicki smiled. "Our boogie boards would work, too."

Soon old pieces of wood, real-estate signs, tyres and chairs dotted the lawn, creating a mismatched but effective collection of jumps.

"We need at least two more," Kelly declared, as she eyed the course. Her eyes lit up when she saw a line of gorse bushes growing at the top of a bank at the far corner of the lawn. "How about we canter up the bank and jump over the gorse?"

Vicki shook her head. "It's too high and wide."

Rolling her eyes, Kelly ran over to the shed and grabbed a pair of hedge-trimmers and gloves. "Seriously, Vicki, where's your imagination?" For the next ten minutes, Vicki and the others watched on as Kelly snipped pieces of gorse, transforming the bushes into a long box hedge about 80 centimetres high.

"That's brilliant," Vicki cried out when her sister had finished. "I just hope I don't fall off and land in the middle of it. The thorns would take days to get out!"

Wincing, Kelly laughed. "I didn't think about that!"

"We just need one more jump," Vicki said as she looked over at Charlie, who was now grazing happily by their A-frame rabbit hutch. As she watched the rabbits darting in and out of their box, an idea formed.

"The rabbit hutch!"

"Did they escape again?" Amanda cried.

"No! But we should jump it."

"There's no way the ponies will jump it," Kelly gasped. "It's huge!"

Vicki's eyes gleamed. "If anyone jumps it clear, they deserve to be the winner!"

∪ ∪ ∪

Once the jumps were made, Vicki and Stella designed a course, carefully planning out the best route to jump around the obstacles.

"Is it going to be like a real show-jumping competition?" Kelly asked.

"Of course," Vicki said.

"Then we'll need a timer to see who jumps around the fastest, and start and finish flags so we know when to start and stop the time."

"Can we put numbers on the jumps, too? Then it'll be just like a real show!" Amanda said as she lifted one of the rabbits from its hutch. "Do you think Floppy will mind the ponies jumping over him?"

Shaking her head, Vicki smiled. "Floppy and Fluffy will be fine — they can always hide in their box if they get worried."

"If I was a rabbit, I'd watch the ponies sailing over me," Amanda declared as she gave Floppy a hug and placed him back into his cage. "It would be way more fun than just eating grass all day!"

"Talking of fun, we better finish this course quickly. Annabelle and Stella's parents will be here in an hour to watch us compete," Vicki said, as she headed towards the house. "Any ideas about what we can use to make the flags and numbers?"

Kelly twisted her ponytail in one hand as she considered this new challenge. "We could make numbers from the plastic lids of old ice-cream containers?"

"Great idea," Vicki said. "And we can use handkerchiefs tied to bamboo stakes as flags."

Within twenty minutes, the course was complete. The girls walked from jump to jump, learning the correct order. Most of the jumps weren't normal by any definition, and at a glance the lawn looked like a junk heap.

"I wish Charlie wasn't sick — he would have

flown over the jumps," Amanda sighed. "But I'm just so glad he's alive, I don't mind only getting to watch."

"I can't imagine any pony in their right mind jumping over these," Kelly said, biting her lip at the thought of having to get Cameo around the homemade course. She was a lot more confident jumping than she had been a year earlier, but she didn't enjoy big jumps the way her sisters did. "Every jump is more colourful and scarier than anything I've seen at shows!"

"Well, hopefully our ponies aren't in their right minds, then," Amanda said cheekily.

Rolling her eyes, Kelly headed away to catch her pony.

Chapter 15
Show Time

As KELLY RETURNED with a brushed and saddled Cameo, Stella's dad, Peter, pulled up in his car.

"I heard there's a massive show on today and the best riders have turned up here to compete," he joked.

Laughing, Stella led her pony over so that she could give her dad a quick hug. "Wait until you see the course! It's on a whole new level."

"I'm looking forward to it," he smiled. "I hear you need an official time-keeper and I happen to have a watch in working order."

"That would be great. The pony that jumps clear in the fastest time will be the winner," Vicki said, walking up with Casper.

Peter's eyes widened and he glanced at his daughter. "Isn't this the Arabian we tried a while back?"

Stella giggled at her dad's shocked expression. "One and the same."

"He was terrifying when we saw him. It's hard to believe he's the same pony!"

"He was pretty awful when we tried him, too," Vicki said quietly, remembering the first time she'd laid eyes on Casper. "But even then I was sure he had a gentle side."

As they chatted, Vicki suddenly realised she was filled with nerves. Building the jumping course had kept her too busy to think about anything else, but now everything was ready she began to worry about what she was about to do.

Apart from Casper, every other pony had competed at shows and won lots of ribbons. She reminded herself that today was just for fun, but couldn't help glancing over at Dandy grazing on the hill, and for a moment wishing she was riding her champion jumping pony instead.

Turning back to Casper, she stroked his neck and silently apologised for her lack of faith in him. Leaping on bareback, she waited for the others to hop onto their own saddled ponies, then she and Casper led the way towards the lawn.

Looking around at Kelly on Cameo, Stella on Diego and Annabelle on Blackie, Vicki hoped Casper wouldn't be too spooky over the jumps — a refusal or an awkward leap over one of the fences could easily mean a fall. As she knew only too well, without a saddle it would be far too easy to slip off Casper's sleek back.

As they rode their ponies past the vegetable garden, Mum was setting down her gardening tools. "How long until the show begins?"

"Give us fifteen minutes to warm up the ponies and show them all the jumps."

Next they passed the chicken coop, where their dad was throwing out the food scraps.

"It's almost show time!" Kelly called out to him.

"I wouldn't miss it for the world," Dad replied, as he ducked away from the rooster chasing him out of the coop and followed them up the driveway. He settled in one of the chairs which were lined up on the lawn, and began chatting with Peter and Mum.

"Those aren't for you to sit on," Amanda giggled. "They're a jump."

"I guess we'd better relocate then," he said, moving everyone off to sit on the bank.

"You can't sit there either," Vicki laughed as she walked Casper up to show him a jump. He spooked and eyed the obstacle warily; she patted him on the neck to reassure him. "We're cantering up the bank and over the gorse hedge."

"That sounds spiky," Dad grimaced, as the adults moved once again. "By the way, if you need an announcer I'm up for the challenge!"

Vicki halted Casper and smiled in delight. "Yes, please! It's starting to feel more and more like a real competition!"

With their time-keeper and announcer in place, it was show time.

∪ ∪ ∪

Kelly and Cameo were first to compete, and Vicki watched closely to see how the young mare would cope around the challenging course. Vicki had helped Kelly train Cameo from scratch just over a year ago. It had been six months since the pair of them had won their class at the Royal Easter Show, and there was a new sense of confidence about them.

"Watch closely, Casper," Vicki urged her pony as her sister cleared the chairs, then turned to the gorse hedge. "If you jump around the course as steady as Cameo, I'll be very happy."

Laughing, her mum walked over. "I don't think any pony alive could be as kind or safe as Cameo. Certainly not your spooky Arabian!"

Vicki groaned in annoyance. Even with all of Casper's improvements, the family still struggled to see past his quirks. "Why can't you love him just the way he is? He doesn't have to be like the other ponies."

"I know that, honey," her mum said, then frowned. "It's just unusual that you can't ride him in a saddle and bridle yet. Doesn't it frustrate you that he's not making progress?"

"Sometimes," Vicki nodded, as Cameo stopped at the rabbit hutch, before circling around and jumping it the second time. "But then I remember that it was only a few months ago that I couldn't even catch him. The fact that I can do everything on him bareback only shows how much he trusts me. If he wanted me on the ground, there's no way I'd be able to stay on him!"

"Good point," Mum said, and affectionately rubbed Casper's head. "Sometimes it's easy to forget how much he's improved."

Chapter 16
Complete Trust

"THAT'S FOUR FAULTS FOR Kelly and Cameo," Dad's voice boomed across the lawn. "Next up are Annabelle and Blackie."

With only two ponies until her turn, Vicki returned her focus to Casper, slowly warming him up. As they trotted in circles, she kept a distracted eye on Annabelle, then Stella, riding. Both girls had trouble as they navigated the course, but eventually cleared every jump, their ponies slowly gaining confidence as they went round.

"Next in the ring is our final combination," Dad

finally called out. "Please put your hands together for Vicki and Casper, her spirited Arabian."

Vicki rolled her eyes at Dad's dramatic introduction, before urging Casper into a canter. Although he'd been spooky when she'd first shown him the jumps, he bravely flew over the first upright and the oxer before approaching the jump made from chairs. Beneath her, Vicki felt him tense and drop back to a trot, but a slight squeeze with her legs encouraged him forward and they continued jumping clear around the course.

With only one jump to go, Vicki approached the rabbit hutch. Floppy and Fluffy had crept out of their box and sat nibbling on grass as they approached. Praying they wouldn't dart for cover and distract Casper at the last second, Vicki urged her pony on.

"Steady, boy," Vicki said, as she saw Floppy twitch his ears, poised to move. They were going too fast, and Vicki knew that if Casper spooked and refused at this speed she'd fall off for sure. Gripping a handful of mane, she held on for dear life. But soon the rabbits were beneath them as Casper soared up and over the hutch.

"Ladies and gentleman, we have a winner!" Vicki heard her dad call out, as she slowed Casper to a walk. "First place goes to Vicki and Casper, the only clear round from our first class of the day."

Grinning, Vicki rode up to her mum to collect a red ribbon, which they'd recycled from other events they'd competed at. Beside her, Kelly and Cameo lined up in second place, and Stella and Diego were third.

"I think we need to handicap you so the rest of us stand a chance," Stella joked after they finished their victory lap.

Laughing, Vicki glanced over at her friend. "I'm game. What were you thinking?"

"If you weren't already riding bareback, I'd make you remove your saddle." Stella shook her head in admiration. "But you already have that disadvantage."

"What about removing the halter and using just a rope, like when you rode to Charlie's rescue this morning?" Amanda suggested, her eyes full of mischief.

"Yes!" Annabelle agreed. "I'd love to watch you ride him like that again — he was so good this morning."

Vicki saw their eager expressions, then glanced down at Casper. He'd certainly been good earlier in the day, but he'd only had to follow behind Cameo — nothing as challenging as jumping around a full course.

"Oh, come on," Kelly begged. "It'd be amazing to see, even if you just jump one or two jumps."

Keen to give it a go, Vicki leapt off Casper's back and removed his halter, then twisted the rope around his muzzle. Vaulting back on, she turned his head to the left and right to make sure she could steer him, then walked him in a circle and halted.

"I think he'll be OK," Vicki grinned.

"You should ride last again," Kelly told her sister. "That way we'll all be able to watch you without having to worry about warming up our ponies."

"Good idea," Stella said. "I don't want to miss it!"

ᴗ ᴗ ᴗ

The girls had agreed that this class would be Take Your Own Line, which meant that the fences could be jumped in any order, and from either direction.

The only rule was that they had to jump everything, and only once.

For ten minutes, Vicki, Kelly, Stella and Annabelle looked at the course, trying to figure out the fastest track to take between the jumps, careful to keep their route top secret in case it gave the others an advantage. Over and over, Vicki made up and discarded potential courses, determined to cover the least possible ground. Finally, she settled on the order.

"I'm sorted," she said confidently. "Good luck trying to beat me."

"There's no way your course is going to be as good as mine," Kelly boasted.

"You girls are dreaming." Stella rolled her eyes. "The route I've come up with is guaranteed to win."

Laughing at their banter, Annabelle put her foot in the stirrups and swung up onto Blackie's back. "Not if I can pull off the angles I have planned. May the best pony win!"

Annabelle rode first, and she jumped a perfect clear round, clocking up a fast time. Next was Stella, and she also jumped faultlessly, although a fraction slower.

"Well, I'm at a disadvantage," Kelly joked when it was her turn. "Everyone's going clear and there's no way Cameo's going to be the fastest!"

As Vicki watched Kelly canter around the jumps, she couldn't help but smile. On style Cameo would certainly have won, but on speed they didn't stand a chance.

"And that's a clear round for Cameo," Dad announced merrily, "but ten seconds slower than the time to beat."

Finally, it was Vicki's turn. She turned Casper to the first jump, flying over it before spinning to the next. Not once did she have to worry about a lack of control as he listened closely for the slightest cue, responsive to the rope. Never had Vicki jumped on such tight angles, but Casper effortlessly navigated the course, quick and nimble on his feet.

"And Casper takes the win — sixteen seconds faster than any of our other competitors," Dad said, his voice croaking in disbelief.

Chapter 17
Straight from the Horse's Mouth

As soon as Vicki slowed Casper down, she was surrounded. Everyone was gushing over how special the pony was, and how amazing he'd been.

"What an exceptional pony," Mike said, congratulating Vicki. "I bet he's won a lot of shows over the years." He'd returned to check on Casper and had arrived in time to see the girls' final class. "And it's amazing that you can ride him bareback and without even a bridle!"

"Oh, he's not a competition pony," Stella laughed.

"Vicki has to ride him like that because he's so dangerous in a saddle or bridle!"

"Really?" Mike said, not sure if she was joking.

"It's true," Vicki said, with a sigh. "He's never been to a show, and probably won't ever compete, because he can't stand wearing a bridle or saddle."

"What does he do?"

"As soon as you put contact on his mouth, he throws his head up or rears."

"He seems far too sweet to be acting badly for no reason," Mike murmured as he gently opened Casper's mouth. "Have you done his teeth?"

"Are we supposed to brush our ponies' teeth every night?" Amanda asked, confused, as she eyed Casper's front teeth.

Mike glanced at Amanda, then laughed. "No," he said, smiling. "But that would be funny!"

"What do you mean, then?" Vicki asked. She was desperate to know why Mike thought Casper's teeth might be causing his bad behaviour.

"Horses can have all sorts of teeth problems, which can make it really painful for them to be ridden, especially with a bit in," he explained. "Ideally, you should have an equine dentist out once a year to give your horses a check-up and make sure there isn't anything causing them pain."

Running a hand inside Casper's mouth, Mike's face became grave. "It feels like he's got lots of issues. You'll need this confirmed by an equine dentist, but I suspect it'll explain why he's a little underweight as well."

"And you really think it could solve his behavioural problems?" Mum asked doubtfully.

"It'll help," Mike said. Pulling a pen from his pocket, he jotted down a phone number and passed it over. "Here's the number for Warwick — he's one of the best equine dentists in the country."

"Mum," said Vicki anxiously, "how will we afford this? I bet equine dentists are really expensive."

Mum looked at Dad, then at Vicki. "We have a little nest egg from the sales of Squizzy, Jude's foal and Twinkle. It was set aside for horse emergencies, so we can use it for Casper's teeth."

"Thank you so much," said Vicki, wrapping Casper in a hug.

It took three weeks to get an appointment with Warwick, and for Vicki the days couldn't pass fast enough. With the show season well underway, though, she had to turn her focus to Dandy, and found that there was plenty to keep her busy.

Each weekend there was a different event for the sisters to compete at, and they were enjoying trying a range of competitions. They rode at a Ribbon Day, then competed in a Mounted Games competition and, in late November, they rode in their first A&P Show of the season. Dandy, Cameo and Charlie were becoming very good all-rounders and their collection of ribbons was growing.

Finally, the day of the dental appointment arrived. Vicki was impatient for school to finish so she could get home and meet the equine dentist. Her sisters were equally excited, and chatted loudly in the car as their mum drove them home.

"Do you think he'll need to have any teeth pulled out?" Kelly asked, shuddering in horror. She'd had a molar pulled out by the dentist when she was younger and still had nightmares about it.

"I hope not," Vicki grimaced. Although she didn't mind the dentist, she couldn't imagine Casper would enjoy having any teeth removed. "I wonder if horses can have fillings?"

As soon as they arrived home, Vicki quickly got changed, then rushed up the hill to catch Casper. She was just in time — Warwick drove up just as she led the Arabian up the driveway.

"So is this the problem pony?" he asked, as he stepped out and patted Casper's head.

"I can't ride him with a bit," Vicki explained. "But he's perfect in a halter."

Warwick set to work checking Casper's front teeth, then he fastened a gag onto the pony's head and cranked his mouth open so he could work on his back teeth. Vicki was impressed by how patiently Casper stood while the dentist filed off the sharp edges.

"He got some major problems, including some teeth that need to be removed, which would explain why he's acting up," Warwick said as he worked. "I can't fix them without sedation, though, so I'll need to come back with a vet."

Vicki turned to her mum. "You should ring and see if Mike's home, then we could sedate him now."

"Great idea," Mum smiled. "It's handy having a vet for a friend!"

Ten minutes later, Mike met them at the yards with his supplies. Within minutes, Casper was sleepy and Warwick set to work again. By the time he was finished, Casper looked a little worse for wear and stood in the yard with his head hanging low, fast asleep.

Warwick gave him a pat and turned to Vicki and Mum. "Keep an eye on him until he wakes up, then give him a few days to recover. Now that his teeth are sorted he should be fine to try riding in a bit, but give me a call if he still has problems."

Chapter 18
A Completely Different Pony

THREE DAYS LATER, VICKI BRIDLED Casper for the first time in months. While she was hopeful he'd behave, secretly she thought it was unlikely that one visit from the dentist would have fixed all of Casper's problems.

"I really hope I don't fall off you again," Vicki told her pony as she leapt onto him. "The last few times we tried this it didn't end well!"

"Let's just stay in the paddock today," Dad said, clearly also a little worried. "That way we can keep an eye on you."

With a click of Vicki's heels, Casper strode eagerly forward, walking on a loose rein. As they circled the paddock, Vicki was careful to keep her hands soft and give Casper time to get used to wearing a bit before she asked him to slow down. She braced herself for trouble — it was when she put pressure on the reins that the problems always began.

Knowing she couldn't put it off forever, Vicki closed her hands on the reins and asked him to stop. Instead of reacting badly, Casper simply dropped back to a halt.

Gazing down at her pony in disbelief, Vicki leaned forward and hugged him. Picking up a trot, she spent the next twenty minutes testing him out. Walk, trot, canter, halt, trot, halt. Not once did Casper misbehave.

"It's just like he's being ridden in a halter!" Vicki said as she rode over to the fence line, where everyone stood watching.

"Wow — all these years of misbehaviour could have been prevented if only he'd had his teeth done," Mum said, slowly shaking her head in disbelief.

Vicki swung off Casper's back and passed the reins to her mum to hold.

"I need to check something else. I've always ridden Casper in a saddle and bridle at the same time, so I assumed he hated all gear. But what if it was his teeth all along and he's actually fine in a saddle?"

"It's worth a try," Dad grinned. "If he copes, you'll be able to start competing him!"

Vicki tried to contain her growing excitement as she sprinted off. Returning a few minutes later, she quickly tacked him up, then swung into the saddle.

With her heart beating a million miles an hour, Vicki asked Casper to walk forward. With every stride he took, Vicki grew more relaxed. Soon she felt confident enough to trot him.

"It's like he's a completely different pony," Kelly whispered in awe, unable to believe the transformation.

Mum gazed proudly at Vicki. "I'm so glad you pestered us to save him. You've changed his life for the better."

"I always knew deep down that he wanted to be good," Vicki said, as she hugged Casper once again. "But it must have been so painful for him every time he got ridden. No wonder he didn't like people anywhere near him."

"Well, fortunately for him, those days are behind him," Dad said. "What's next in his story, I wonder?"

A wide smile split Vicki's face. Her eyes sparkled as she gazed at Casper. "I think he's ready for the Pony Club Trek!"

Chapter 19
Pony Club Trek

THE NEXT MONTH WENT QUICKLY, with Christmas and New Year passing in a blur. The annual Pony Club Trek was Vicki's favourite event of the summer, and this would be her third time attending. The whole family would be camping at the beach for a week in January, with all five of their ponies, and most of their friends would be there, too.

In the days leading up to the trek there was lots of work to be done, and Vicki and her sisters spent hours cleaning their gear and packing.

"Do you think Casper will cope with so many

other horses?" Kelly asked, as they carried their horse gear to the truck. There would be over a hundred horses at the trek, and on the first day everyone had to ride for several hours to get to the beachfront property where they would be camping.

"He's been so good at Pony Club rallies over the past few weeks," Vicki said, smiling. "But it'll still be a huge deal for him. I doubt he's ever been ridden on the beach or swum in the sea, and he certainly hasn't competed in formation rides or games days."

Amanda screwed up her face. "I thought you'd ride Dandy in the competitions. Wouldn't he have a better chance of winning?"

"Probably, but I thought it would be good life experience for Casper. I'll ride Dandy on the beach each day and swim him in the estuary, though."

"He'll enjoy that," Amanda grinned.

"Are you going to ride out on the trek this year?" Vicki asked her. Normally the youngest riders trucked their ponies to the property.

"Mum finally said I could," Amanda said with delight, as she rummaged through the tack shed in search of brushes and a hoof pick to take with them. "I can't wait."

The morning of the trek dawned bright and clear, and the truck was loaded in record time. Since the Wilsons' truck fitted only three ponies at a time, and there were five ponies to transport, they headed off early so their parents would have time to make two trips. Casper, Cameo, Charlie and the girls would be dropped at the starting point, a woolshed, so they could ride out on the trek with everyone else, then Mum and Dad would return home for Dandy and Jude, drive them to the beach and settle them in paddocks before setting up their campsite.

From the moment they arrived at the woolshed, everyone moved at full speed. The girls saddled their ponies as fast as possible — with the exception of Casper, as Vicki had decided to ride out bareback. Although he was fine in a saddle now, Vicki still preferred to ride him without one, especially since he was no longer as bony.

Soon they were mounted and joined the growing collection of riders. Every Pony Club in the region was attending, so there were many people the girls didn't recognise, but occasionally they saw someone from their own branch.

"Hey, Stella — over here!" Vicki yelled, when she saw Diego standing off to one side. Waving in greeting, Stella made her way over to join them.

"Who's ready to ride?" a loud voice rang out across the paddock. In front of the yards, a man was sitting astride a giant black horse. Looking around, Vicki noticed that she was the only one riding bareback.

The man on the black horse gazed out over the group, and when he saw Vicki a frown flickered over his face. Spurring his horse forward, he rode over to her.

"It's a long, tough ride," the man cautioned. "Do you think you'll be able to keep up bareback?"

Vicki smiled confidently. "When I was younger, I learnt to ride bareback because we couldn't afford a saddle. I ride Casper like this all the time, so it actually feels more comfortable this way."

The man's eyes challenged her, but Vicki bravely held his gaze.

"No crying, then, and make sure you keep up," he finally conceded, as he spun his horse and trotted off.

Chapter 20
Tougher Stuff

THE FIRST PART OF THE RIDE went well, walking and trotting over gentle rolling hills, and Vicki soon forgot the man's stern warning. The ponies were enjoying themselves and didn't seem bothered by the other horses, as the girls rode along at the back of the group. Soon the terrain became steeper and the pace faster, however.

Those in front of the pack, which the man on the black horse was leading, would canter up every hill, but because they were at the back the girls were often still walking down the previous hill as the horses in front began cantering up the next one. Excited by the commotion, their ponies began jig-jogging and tugging on the reins, and a few times they slipped as they made their way down narrow, steep tracks.

Kelly's eyes welled up with tears. "We should have gone in the truck! Can I hop off and lead Cameo?"

Worried about falling behind and getting lost, Vicki shook her head.

"I think they're only excited because we're trying to make them walk. On the next hill let's just let them canter down, so they can keep up with everyone else, then we'll gallop up the next one as fast as possible to get to the front of the group."

Luckily, the next hill was not too steep, and Vicki led the charge, weaving between riders as they cantered down the hill in an attempt to overtake the other horses. By the time they reached the bottom they were in the middle of the pack, and they kicked their ponies on, flying up the hill on the other side.

When they rode up alongside the big black horse, the leader turned and looked at them in shock. Vicki couldn't help but grin.

"You girls are riding well," he said, with renewed respect. "I thought you'd have fallen off by now, or be crying at the back of the group."

Vicki glanced at Kelly, relieved that her tears had dried. "We're made of tougher stuff than that."

∪ ∪ ∪

Now they were at the front, their ponies returned to a relaxed walk, without pulling on the reins or trying to jig-jog. As Vicki had hoped, they were able to walk down every hill, then canter calmly up the other side. By the time they reached the estuary they had to cross, the girls had almost forgotten about the scarier parts of the ride and were having the time of their lives.

"Oh, look!" Amanda cried out. "There's Mum and Dad."

Sure enough, their parents and Stella's dad were waiting for them by the water's edge. The tide was too high to ride the ponies across without swimming, so their parents had gathered to help unsaddle their horses and carry the gear on foot across a long, narrow walking bridge that spanned the estuary.

"You guys made record time! How was the ride?"

Dad asked, as he loosened Cameo's girth.

Kelly pulled off her riding boots and socks, so they wouldn't get wet. "It was the best ride ever! A little scary in the middle maybe, but mostly fun!"

Mum's eyebrows rose. "No one fell off, though, right?"

"No, the ponies were good. They're a bit hot and sweaty, though, so they'll enjoy a swim."

Dad gave them each a leg up and they rode their

ponies into the water, keeping near the front of the group. The first part was only knee-deep, and Casper eagerly splashed through the shallow water. As soon as they reached the channel, though, it rapidly got deeper, and Charlie, who was the smallest by far, was soon swimming. A few metres later, the rest of their ponies were also out of their depth.

Casper kept trying to circle back, to get his feet back on solid ground, and it took all of Vicki's strength to keep him swimming straight. Beside her, Cameo and Charlie had their ears pricked forward and were intent on the far shore — they had both crossed this estuary many times and knew that they'd be on dry land soon enough.

As soon as Casper's hooves touched the far shoreline, Vicki breathed a sigh of relief. It was always stressful swimming ponies across the estuary for the first time. They rode across the paddock to where her parents had set up camp, and Vicki gave her tired pony a pat.

Vicki fell into bed that night exhausted. As well as the long ride that day, she had had too many sleepless nights the week before, tossing and turning in her excitement about the trek.

As she lay listening to the ponies nickering outside in the paddocks surrounding the campsite, she thought back over the ride out, proud of how well Casper had behaved. It had been a big day for him, and with a whole week of camp before them, there was plenty more fun ahead.

Chapter 21
Fun and Games

THE NEXT MORNING VICKI WOKE early and ran down to visit the ponies. They were all grazing together, along with Diego, in the pine paddock on the hill. As soon as Casper and Dandy saw her, they neighed out and trotted over for a pat. Vicki felt like the luckiest girl in the world to own two such beautiful ponies.

After feeding them a carrot each, she heard a bell toll in the distance. She'd lost track of time and was going to be late for the morning meeting! Sprinting back the way she had come, she hurried over to the circle of people sitting listening to the president of the local Pony Club talk over the plan for the day.

"What did I miss?" Vicki whispered when she found her family.

"There's a fast beach ride at ten, and a slow one at eleven-thirty," Dad replied.

Vicki smiled, pleased both her ponies would be able to ride out on the beach. Since Casper would be tired after his huge ride the day before, she'd take him with the slower group. That way, Dandy could go for a gallop and stretch his legs on the 10 a.m. ride.

"And don't forget to enter for the dressage formation ride before Thursday," said the president, to finish. "You'll need teams of four, and we're expecting you to have a four-minute dressage test, complete with costumes and music."

Around the circle, people started talking excitedly. Vicki could barely hear over the buzz.

"Have you entered us yet?" Stella asked. They'd been planning their formation ride for weeks. It was one of their favourite events, and they loved coming up with costumes and complicated moves to impress the judges.

"You'll have to find a fourth person," Mum said, looking over at Amanda, who was sitting with three little girls her own age. "Amanda's just decided to do a Beach Babes theme with all her friends, since they have matching white ponies."

Vicki sighed. Teaching someone all the moves in just two days was going to be hard.

"What about Aimee?" Kelly suggested. She was in the same level as them at Pony Club, and had a beautiful bay pony which would match Diego — and the formation ride always looked better when the ponies were the same colour. "That way we'll have two greys and two bays."

"Good idea. If she's keen, we should practise this afternoon."

Aimee was excited about joining their team, so Vicki hurried over to enter them before grabbing her halter and heading back up the hill to catch Dandy.

∪ ∪ ∪

An hour later, as she rode Dandy along the ocean beach in a group of 30 horses and ponies, Vicki couldn't help but smile. Although she loved competing and jumping, nothing beat the freedom of galloping alongside the crashing surf.

"You love the beach as much as I do, don't you, Dandy?" she murmured, as they crossed back over the estuary and made their way back to the truck. The ride had taken much longer than she'd thought, and as she rounded the corner she saw Jude, Cameo and Charlie tied up to the truck, already tacked up. Even Casper had been caught and was standing patiently waiting for her, with his bridle on.

"The next ride leaves in five minutes," Dad said as Vicki jumped off. "I'll put Dandy away so you don't miss out."

The next two days were full of beach riding, swimming in the estuary, playing softball, farm riding, practising their formation ride with Aimee and competing in a Mounted Games competition. Vicki, Stella, Kelly and Amanda made up a team for the games, calling themselves the Kamo Kids after their Pony Club and decorating their ponies with yellow and black, their Pony Club colours.

Unsure which pony to ride, Vicki finally settled on Casper for the team events; and they competed in the sack, bending, mug and sword races, gaining confidence with every competition. Finally, it was time for the barrel race, and Vicki was thrilled to find out she could ride both ponies. Casper's score would count towards the team points, but she could also ride Dandy as an individual.

"We're up first," she told Casper as the barrels were set. The teams would ride first, their score counting for both the teams and individual prizes. While she waited, her eyes traced around the pattern she had to ride. Beneath her, Casper felt calm and sure.

When the time-keeper raised a flag, Vicki urged Casper forward into a canter. Soon the last barrel was behind them, and Vicki settled low over Casper's back as he galloped to the finish line.

"He looked like a pro out there," Mum said, as Casper slowed to a walk beside them.

Vicki leant forward and ruffled Casper's mane. "He loved it! I can't believe how good he's been today."

"He's becoming quite the all-rounder," Dad said, patting Casper's neck. "Hard to believe it's the same angry pony we first met in the winter."

With Casper finished for the day, Vicki handed him over to her mum, then hurriedly hopped on Dandy to compete in the individual competition. She returned to the ring just in time to watch Amanda and Charlie canter around the barrels. Although Charlie was fast for a little pony, he was still much slower than Casper had been.

"What's the winning time?" Vicki asked after she'd warmed up Dandy. They were the last combination left to ride, and Vicki was confident he had a good chance of winning the trophy for the fastest individual time.

"You are," Kelly beamed. "No one's managed to beat the time you set on Casper!"

As Vicki waited for her second turn, she was torn. If she rode a fraction slower on Dandy, Casper was guaranteed the win and it would be all the more special because it would be his first ever ribbon and trophy. But that wouldn't be fair on Dandy, who also deserved the chance to do his best.

As the flag raised, she knew what she had to do. Kicking Dandy forward, they cantered towards the first barrel, the ground whizzing by in a blur as they circled the three barrels in rapid succession. As they rode over the finish line, Dandy tossed his head in enjoyment and Vicki was filled with pride. She had no idea which pony had won, but she'd given them both her best effort, and that was all she could do.

"First we have the winners of the team events," the announcer's voice rang out as Vicki hurriedly swapped ponies. "The winning team for the barrel race is Kamo Kids!" Vicki smiled at her team members as they all rode their ponies forward to receive their red ribbons. Next, the ribbons for the rest of the team games were presented, and soon Casper's neck was decorated in a colourful array of ribbons — the Kamo Kids had also placed in the bending, flag and sack races. Vicki was so proud of how well Casper had coped at his first event.

Finally, the judge called forward the winners for the most prestigious class of the day, the individual barrel race. "And the winner of the Barrel Race Trophy, for the fastest individual time, goes to Vicki Wilson and Just Fine n Dandy, with her other pony, Casper, in second place!"

Swapping onto Dandy, Vicki rode him forward, leading Casper, so neither pony would miss out on getting their well-deserved prize.

Chapter 22
Dressage Divas

THE MORNING OF THE DRESSAGE formation ride was hectic. In every direction, teams were decorating their horses for the themed event. Teams would be judged not only for Best Performance, but also for Best Presented, so the girls woke early to groom their horses until they shone, and to plait their manes.

"At least we didn't have to wash them," Kelly said with relief. "All that swimming in the salt water has kept them so clean."

"I've never seen Casper so white!" Vicki agreed, as she brushed out her pony's tail.

"I wish we lived closer to the beach," Amanda said, as she fitted a life-jacket around her pony's neck. "Charlie's impossible to keep clean normally."

With her little pony ready, she headed into the truck to get dressed into her own costume — swimsuit, flippers, goggles and a snorkel — before laying a towel over Charlie's back and jumping on.

"I'm off to find the rest of the Beach Babes," she said with a queenly wave.

Vicki struggled to contain a laugh as her little sister rode off, then turned back to Casper. The event would start in half an hour, and they still had a few finishing touches left to make before changing into their own costumes for their Spice Girls-themed routine.

"Hurry up, Kelly," Vicki demanded as she banged on the truck door.

"I feel ridiculous," Kelly grumbled as she stepped down the ramp, wearing a little black dress and high heels. "Why couldn't *I* be Sporty Spice?"

Vicki laughed as she ducked inside the truck to get changed into track pants and a sports top, her hair tied up in a ponytail. "Because there was no way I was going to wear a dress!"

As they swung up onto their horses, Stella rode up in a leopard-print jumpsuit, with a frizzy black wig.

"Even Scary Spice would have been better," Kelly complained.

Aimee soon joined them dressed as Baby Spice, her long blonde hair in pigtails. "At least you don't have to wear a pink dress!" Vicki joked to Kelly.

U U U

Seventeen teams had entered, and the Spice Girls were drawn to ride fourteenth. With plenty of time till the four girls were due in the ring, they dismounted and held their ponies while they watched the first eight teams.

Some had opted to wear their Pony Club uniforms, while others had gone all out. There were nuns, clowns, dragons, class nerds, bumblebees and pirates.

"The standard's pretty high this year," Dad commented as he watched four horses in the ring complete a complicated move. "Every year it just gets better and better."

Vicki couldn't help but agree. It was one of the most competitive events of the season, and many of the riders spent months planning for it.

"Oh, look, Amanda's team is next," Mum said, grabbing her camera and snapping photos as they began their routine. They were the youngest riders, on the smallest ponies, and the crowd loved them.

"It's cute that they all rode bareback." Mum winked at Vicki. "I wonder who inspired them?"

Vicki grinned as she looked over at Casper. "Lots of good has come from those troublesome first few months, but I am so relieved those days are behind me!"

"Me, too," Mum agreed. "Every time you went near him I was terrified that you'd get hurt."

Vicki paused and glanced back at her mum. "I didn't realise that."

"I didn't want my fear to rub off on you. You wouldn't have made any progress with him if you'd been scared every time you worked him."

Vicki considered her mum's words thoughtfully. "I guess at the beginning there were a few moments when he scared me, but not any more."

The horn hooted, signalling their turn. Vicki glanced sideways at the others to see if they were ready. With a small nod, she closed her legs against Casper's sides and squeezed him into a trot.

In perfect formation, to the opening bars of the Spice Girls song 'Stop', they entered the arena and trotted down the centre line, halting to salute the judge. Then they performed a series of intricate movements they'd invented, many that had never been seen before in the competition.

To finish, Kelly, Stella and Aimee trotted up the centre line and Vicki came up from behind, weaving between them at a canter, before all four riders turned, side-by-side, and began a spiralling figure of eight pattern, and saluted the judge.

"That was our best performance," Stella squealed as they left the ring. "The horses were perfect!"

As Vicki watched the last three teams ride, she was confident they stood a good chance of placing. The judges loved originality, and her team had pulled off every new move they'd dreamt up.

Finally it was time for the prizegiving, and everyone lined up across the paddock. As all sixty-eight horses got into position, Vicki looked around her, overwhelmed by the number of riders that had competed. Most were much older than them, and there were even a few teams made up of adults.

First, the winners were called forward for Best Presented. Some of the more dramatic costumes placed, and Vicki was pleased to see the clowns, who were from her Pony Club, win. She knew just how much time had gone into making their costumes.

Next the judge called out the placegetters for the best performance. Then, "In second place, we have . . . the Spice Girls!"

Aimee shrieked, and together the four girls rode forward to collect their blue ribbons.

"And the crowd favourites and the overall winners of the formation ride are . . . the Beach Babes!"

Vicki and Kelly gazed in disbelief as their little sister rode forward with her friends. Amanda and her friends were all just seven years old, and had decided to compete only a few days earlier.

Amanda wore the same shocked expression as her sisters. "But we didn't even canter!" she could be heard saying to the judge as she congratulated them.

"No, but you made up for that by riding bareback," the judge grinned as she handed over the coveted trophy. "I thought you were all outstanding!"

As Amanda held the trophy up to the cheering crowd, Vicki rolled her eyes in amusement. Perhaps the Spice Girls should have ridden bareback, too!

But she was filled with pride, and satisfied by her own performance. Standing side by side with the other Spice Girls, Vicki thought about those early days when things were going wrong with Casper. How differently his story would have ended if she hadn't given him a second chance.

And later, as the girls headed to the estuary to cool off their ponies with a swim, Vicki realised just how much Casper had taught her. Not all ponies were naughty on purpose — sometimes bad behaviour could be a pony's way of showing that something hurt. She leant down and wrapped her arms around Casper's graceful neck. She had a feeling that her spirited Arabian still had plenty more to teach her!

Casper

Braeburn Casper was born in 1993 and came to live with us in the autumn of 1998.

Under Vicki's love and guidance, the 14.1-hand, grey Arabian gelding transformed into a highly successful and trustworthy all-rounder, proving that every pony deserves a second chance. By the end of their first season together Vicki and Casper had won their first Champion Hunter and went on to compete in show jumping, games, cross country and dressage competitions.

Although he won innumerable champions, Vicki's favourite memories are of riding him bareback at home, using only her voice and legs to guide him. She trusted Casper with her life and accomplished things with him she'd previously only dreamed of.

Casper lived with our family for many years, before the Bennetts convinced us to let him retire to their farm. He lives there to this day and has taught countless kids to ride.

Characters

Vicki has always shown talent for riding, training and competing with horses. She has won national titles and championships in Showing, Show Hunter and Show Jumping, and has represented New Zealand internationally. Dandy was the first pony she trained, when she was nine years old, and then twenty years later she won the World Championships for Colt Starting. When she's not riding, she loves to learn as much about horses as she can, from farriers, vets, physios and dentists.

Kelly has always been creative. She loves horses, photography and writing. Although she competed to Grand Prix level when she was sixteen, she now

only show jumps for fun, and also enjoys taming
wild horses. Her favourite rides are out on the
farm, swimming in the river, or cantering down
the beach. When she's not on a horse, she is very
daring, and loves going on extreme adventures.

Amanda is the family comedian and can always
make people laugh! As a child she was always
pulling pranks and getting up to mischief. Amanda
began show jumping at a young age, and competed
in her first Grand Prix when she was twelve. In
2010, she won the Pony of the Year, the most
prestigious Pony Grand Prix in the Southern
Hemisphere, and since then she has had lots of
wins up to World Cup level. When she's not
outside training her horses or teaching other riders,
Amanda loves doing something creative — she has
already filmed two documentaries, and is writing
her first book.

Mum (Heather Wilson) grew up with a love of
horses, although she was the only one in her family
to ride. She volunteered at a local stable from the
age of thirteen, teaching herself to ride when she

was gifted an injured racehorse. Although she rides only occasionally now, her love of horses hasn't faded over the years, and she is always ringside to watch her daughters compete. In her spare time, Heather loves painting and drawing anything to do with horses, and as 'Camp Mum' is popular with the young riders who attend Showtym Camps.

Dad (John Wilson) grew up with horses, hunting, playing polo and riding on the farm. His family also show jumped and trained steeplechasers, so he has loved horses from a young age. He hurt his back when he was in his twenties, which has limited his horse riding, but he enjoys watching his daughters ride and is very proud of their success. When he's not fixing things around the farm, he can be found gardening or creating stunning life-sized horse sculptures from recycled horseshoes.

How-tos

The most important thing about owning a pony is to learn as much as you can about their care and training, so you can make their life as fun and easy as possible! In each book in the *Showtym Adventures* series, we will expand on key lessons Vicki, Amanda and I learnt on our journey to becoming better horse riders. Some lessons we learnt by making mistakes; others from observing our horses and learning from them — and some knowledge has been passed down to us by others. We hope you enjoy these top tips!

How to ride bareback

As kids we learnt to ride bareback out of necessity because our parents couldn't afford to buy us saddles. The balance we gained in those early years gave us a great foundation, and even to this day we often ride bareback, including the very first ride on our young horses when we start their training.

At one Ribbon Day, when I was only seven years old, we forgot the girth for my saddle so I had to compete bareback. The judge couldn't believe it and I remember placing third in my rider class. Back then, riding bareback was quite common and at most A&P shows there was a Bareback Rider over Hurdles class — which Vicki, Amanda and I frequently won. I still remember the raised eyebrows when Vicki competed bareback in a Grand Prix show-jumping class on her horse Witheze in 2009, and the thousands of spectators that were amazed by her jumping 1.82 metres bareback in the 2011 Horse of the Year Puissance on Showtym Girl.

Riding bareback improves your skills as a rider, fine-tunes your balance, improves your stickability and enhances your communication with your horse, so it's a valuable skill to gain if you're serious about your riding. On the following pages we've outlined some of the key benefits to riding bareback and some of our top tips so that you can give it a go.

Benefits of riding bareback

- Bareback riding is a great way to develop your strength as a rider. Without a saddle to support you, you must rely on your legs and core to keep yourself upright and on the horse.

- Bareback riding truly tests your balance and will help identify areas where your position can be improved, helping you to move more in tune with your pony's movements.

- Bareback riding allows you to feel your horse's muscles moving and shifting beneath you, developing your awareness of how your horse's body moves and reacts when you shift your weight.

- Bareback riding will increase your stickability, making it easier to stay on the next time your horse spooks or bolts under saddle. Because you're able to feel your pony's muscles shifting, it's also easier to anticipate when something is about to go wrong, often avoiding potential accidents.

Top tips for riding bareback

- Before you begin, be sure you have mastered the halt, turning, walk, trot and canter in the saddle, with and without stirrups.

- Mounting your pony bareback, without the aid of stirrups, can be difficult. The best way is to learn how to vault or jump onto your pony bareback, but in the meantime a mounting block, or having someone to give you a leg up, works just as well.

- A good position in the saddle is the same when riding bareback. The alignment from your ear, shoulder, hip and heel should form a straight line — see the illustration on page 161.

- Mastering the sitting trot in the saddle will help your balance when trotting bareback for the first time. Keep your legs long and heels down. Think of letting your weight sink down through your 'seat cushions' and legs.

- If you start to lose your balance, don't clench the horse with your legs. Your pony could understand this as a cue to move faster.

- Whatever you do, don't use the reins for balance. That will confuse and hurt your pony, especially if they're wearing a bit.

- Going up hills or banks can be a challenge bareback.

Lean forward to get your weight off your pony's back and use handfuls of mane to stop sliding backwards.

- When you first start trotting and cantering bareback it can help to have someone lunge your pony; that way you don't have to worry about controlling your pony, and can concentrate on maintaining your seat.

Bareback riding position

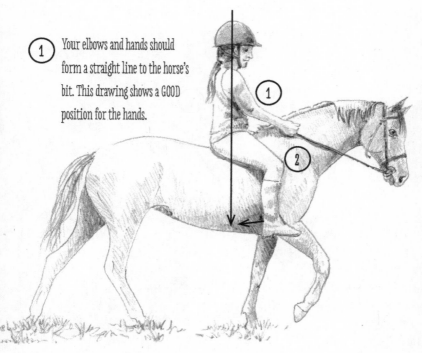

1. Your elbows and hands should form a straight line to the horse's bit. This drawing shows a GOOD position for the hands.

2. Your shoulders, hips and heels should form a straight line to ensure your centre of gravity is correct. This drawing shows a POOR position as the rider's feet are too far forward.

Jumping bareback

1. Hands: when jumping, your hands should stay soft and there should be a crease in the reins to ensure you don't pull on the horse's mouth.

2. Head: you should be looking up, in the direction that you are riding in, which will help your horse stay straight and balanced.

3. Legs: a good leg position should be the same with or without a saddle, with the lower leg on the girth area for balance.

Glossary

A&P Show agricultural and pastoral fair with displays of
livestock and farming equipment, entertainment, food
stalls and competitions — including show jumping.

Arabian an ancient horse breed from the Arabian Peninsula,
known for their distinctive heads, speed and intelligence.

barrel race a horse and rider race around a series of barrels.
Whoever gets around the course in the fastest time —
without knocking over any barrels — is the winner.

bit the metal mouthpiece of a bridle.

bridle gear placed on the horse's head — including the bit
and reins — that is used to direct and guide the animal.

browbands the strap on the bridle which goes over the
horse's brow or forehead. Browbands can be plain leather
or include bright decorations.

buck a bucking horse jumps and arches its back, which
makes it very hard for the rider to stay on.

bush, the a New Zealand word for the forest.

canter the horse gait between a trot and a gallop.

colic abdominal pain in a horse. Always call your
veterinarian if you think your horse has colic as it can be
very serious.

crossbars a simple horse jump with a horizontal bar raised on two vertical posts. The height of the horizontal bar can be adjusted according to how high a horse can jump.

dished a head shape similar to a seahorse, which is common in Arabian horses.

dressage a form of horse training where horse and rider work together to learn a collection of particular movements — a bit like dance! In competitions, horses are judged on their balance, movement and obedience.

farm a ranch where livestock are raised.

faults penalties given during show-jumping competitions — for example, if a horse refuses to jump or knocks over a rail.

float a horse float, a horse carrier that is hitched up to a separate vehicle.

formation ride a competition in which several riders and their horses must ride together in a particular routine.

gait the way a horse moves; a walk, trot, canter or gallop.

gallop the fastest horse gait.

gelding a castrated male horse.

girth a cinch, the band that secures the saddle to a horse.

Grand Prix show jumping the top level of show jumping.

hand ponies and horses are measured in 'hands'. One hand equals 4 inches (10.16cm).

halt to come to a stop.

halter a harness for a horse's head, used to lead the horse.

hunter class event a competition in which a horse and rider must navigate a course of fences.

jig-jog between a walk and a slow trot, a jig-jogging horse is very uncomfortable to ride. Horses jig-jog for a number of different reasons including anxiety or excitement.

jump standard the standards on each side of the jump, used to adjust the jump height.

jumper a sweater.

lead rein (rope) the rope used to guide a horse.

mane the hair that grows on the top ridge of a horse's neck.

muzzle the nose and jaws of a horse.

nicker a relatively quiet vibrating noise, which the horse makes with its mouth closed, usually as a sign of affection.

oxer a jump with two horizontal rails set across from each other with a gap between. This makes the jump wider and more challenging for the horse.

paddock a pasture or field of grass where horses are kept.

pick out (hooves) to clear a horse's hooves of stone and debris.

pony small horse breeds that are under 14.2 hands tall.

rear a horse throws its head up and stands on its hind legs when rearing. This can be very dangerous for a rider as they can easily fall off the horse.

Ribbon Day a day of competitions where ribbons are awarded as prizes to the winners.

Royal Easter Show an annual event held at Easter with carnival rides, agricultural events, live music, food stalls and sporting events.

rugged to cover a horse in a rug to protect them from extreme weather conditions.

supermarket grocery store.

tack horse equipment.

trek riding a pony or horse across country, also known as trail riding.

trot the gait between a walk and a canter.

truck a horse truck, a vehicle and horse carrier in one.

unbroken a horse that has not been trained and is therefore not safe to ride.

walk the slowest horse gait.

withers the bony ridge between a horse's shoulder blades, at the bottom of the neck. The height of a horse is measured from the withers to the ground.

woolshed a large shed on a farm, used for shearing sheep.

Thank you

AT THE TIME, THE LESSONS we learnt from Casper seemed ground-breaking. The way his behaviour changed after having his teeth done was obvious, and it was a relief to be able to offer him a more comfortable and happier life.

In the twenty years since then, our knowledge about sore and difficult horses has grown extensively. Each problem pony we encountered (and there have been many of them) began a quest to search for solutions to their behavioural issues, rather than punishing them for misbehaving. In hindsight we missed many diagnoses, and there are countless horses that we could have helped if only we'd stumbled across the answer sooner.

Books, manuals, theses and magazine articles became our constant companions, and every time we paid a professional to care for our ponies we used it as an opportunity to ask questions and learn from them. Over the years, the pieces of knowledge gleaned from vets, equine dentists, farriers and physios began to come together to form a picture of horse behaviour which showed us how pain can affect these creatures.

While Amanda and I paid little attention in the early days, both Mum and our older sister, Vicki, were committed to learning as much as possible. Later, when our own interest in horse welfare grew, they were always ready to share their knowledge. For that we are thankful.

Like most lessons, the ones that stayed with us were gained through first-hand experience. Of the hundreds of horses and ponies that have come into our lives, there have been a number of issues to resolve. From horses with poorly fitting saddles and dental issues like Casper's, to skeletal damage and bone splints, to colic, fencing wounds, tetanus and poisoning, we have never been short of learning opportunities.

The most important lesson has been to understand the way in which horses communicate, for although they cannot speak, they are always trying to show us what is wrong. Bucking, kicking, biting, rearing and bolting are only some of the many ways in which our horses have shown their discomfort over the years. The subtler ways, like pinning their ears back, wrinkling their muzzle, showing the whites of their eyes, swishing a tail or holding their body tense are all things we've learnt to watch out for.

So thank you to our horses, for constantly teaching us about themselves. We hope that after a lifetime of learning we will be even closer to understanding these wonderful creatures so that we can strive to give them the best life imaginable.

As always, thanks must also go to my family. Without them, these books wouldn't be possible. Mum and Dad, thank you for the childhood you gave us — I hope one day my own kids can be as free and fun-loving as we were, enjoying the great outdoors like we did, rather than depending on technology for their entertainment. I value the lifestyle we grew up with and wish every child could experience the benefits of living in close contact with animals and nature.

Thanks also to my sisters, the best sidekicks any girl could wish for. So many of the adventures we had as children are still part of our everyday lives. I love the nostalgia of riding bareback, swimming our ponies at the beach, caring for sick and injured animals, galloping over the farm, riding in the dark, making jumps and obstacles out of odds and ends and rescuing horses that others see no value in. Although twenty years have passed since the events described in this book, we are fundamentally the same and take pleasure in the simple things in life. I hope that never changes.

DID YOU ENJOY THIS BOOK?

We love hearing from readers! Here's what some of you have told us about *Dandy, the Mountain Pony*

"First day with Dandy and can't put it down!!" — Madi

"I loved it so much." — Ruby

"I absolutely loved it to pieces. It has inspired me that girls can do anything and dreams really can come true if you want them to. It was a fantastic book. I would rate it 1,000,000,000,000,000,000,000,000,000, stars and even more! Please make more books because I am very excited for the next one."
— Augustine

"*Dandy, the Mountain Pony* had such a friendly vibe to it that made me not want to put the book down! I felt like I was really there watching the action and willing them to succeed." — Charlotte

"I'm 11 years old. Nana bought me the book about Vicki's story of *Dandy, the Mountain Pony* . . . on the 2nd chapter I was picturing about what was happening and I hope that I follow in your footsteps with horses." — Evelyn

"I have finished reading *Dandy, the Mountain Pony* and it's truly amazing. I keep reading it over and over." — Nikita

"I cannot wait until I can read *Cameo, the Street Pony!*" — Sienna

ABOUT THE AUTHOR

© Kelly Wilson

Kelly Wilson is an award-winning photographer and designer, and the bestselling author of four non-fiction books, *For the Love of Horses*, *Stallion Challenges*, *Mustang Ride* and *Saving the Snowy Brumbies*; a picture book, *Ranger the Kaimanawa Stallion*; and the *Showtym Adventures* series. With her sisters Vicki and Amanda, Kelly has starred in the hit-rating TV series, *Keeping up with the Kaimanawas*, following their work taming New Zealand's wild Kaimanawa horses, and has travelled to America and Australia to rescue and tame wild horses.

www.wilsonsisters.co.nz

Have you read . . . Book 1 in the
Showtym Adventures series?

DANDY, THE MOUNTAIN PONY

Let the adventure begin . . . taming a WILD pony!

When nine-year-old Vicki Wilson's beloved lease pony is sold, she is heartbroken. Her family doesn't have much money, and she is desperate to have a pony of her own so she can keep riding.

Then Vicki has the chance she has been waiting for, to tame and train her own wild pony! How will she earn the trust of her beautiful new chestnut? And will Dandy ever be quiet enough for her to ride at Pony Club or compete at Ribbon Days?

This book is inspired by the Wilson Sisters' early years, where Vicki, Kelly and Amanda Wilson first encounter horses in the wild and learn what it takes to make them into champions.

Have you read . . . Book 2 in the
Showtym Adventures series?

CAMEO, THE STREET PONY

The adventure continues : . . training a street pony into a show pony!

When nine-year-old Kelly Wilson outgrows her pony, her mum surprises her with a beautiful steel-grey mare that she spotted trotting down the street, tied to the back of a truck. But there's a catch. Cameo has never been ridden!

While her sisters Vicki and Amanda are jumping higher than ever before, Kelly must face her fears on an untested pony. Will Cameo ever be ready for competitions? And will the girls' ponies hold their own against the purebreds at the Royal Show?

This exciting story of setbacks and success, in which Vicki, Kelly and Amanda Wilson first experience the thrill of serious competition, is inspired by the Wilson Sisters' early years.

Coming next . . . Don't miss Book 4 in the
Showtym Adventures series

CHESSY, THE WELSH PONY

Diamonds in the rough — will these unwanted ponies find love?

Seven-year-old Amanda Wilson dreams of training her own wild pony, just as her big sisters have done. Then comes the chance she has been waiting for — a muster of beautiful Welsh ponies that have run wild in the hills.

Among them is Chessy, a striking stallion, and just the right size for Amanda. But small doesn't equal easy, and first Amanda must prove she has what it takes by training Magic, a stroppy mare from Pony Club. Will Magic and Chessy ever be safe enough to join Amanda on her crazy adventures?

Vicki and Kelly must help Amanda to win her ponies' trust in this engaging story of perseverance and reward, which is inspired by the Wilson Sisters' early years.